MW01105313

Make Me a Home

Make Me a Home

by Tamra Norton

Bonneville Books
Springville, Utah

The views expressed within this work are the sole responsibility of the author and do not necessarily reflect the position of Cedar Fort, Inc., or any other entity.

This is a work of fiction. The characters, names, incidents, places, and dialogue are products of the author's imagination, and are not to be construed as real.

ISBN: 978-1-59955-113-5

Published by Bonneville Books, an imprint of Cedar Fort, Inc., 2373 W. 700 S., Springville, UT, 84663
Distributed by Cedar Fort, Inc. www.cedarfort.com

LIBRARY OF CONGRESS CATALOGING-IN-PUBLICATION DATA

Norton, Tamra, 1964–
 Make me a home / Tamra Norton.
  p. cm.
 Summary: Since moving to Edna, Idaho, to live with her grand-mother while her father is serving in Iraq, twelve-year-old Allie struggles with missing her father and her lack of friends until the day Ivy transfers to her school.
 ISBN 978-1-59955-113-5
 [1. Children of military personnel—Fiction. 2. Separation (Psychology)—Fiction. 3. Best friends—Fiction. 4. Friendship—Fiction. 5.
Family life—Idaho—Fiction. 6. Idaho—Fiction.] I. Title.
 PZ7.N8255Mak 2008
 [Fic]—dc22
                    2007040731

Cover design by Angela Olsen
Cover design © 2008 by Lyle Mortimer
Edited by Kimiko M. Hammari

Printed in the United States of America
10 9 8 7 6 5 4 3 2 1

Printed on acid-free paper.

Dedication

For the children of our valiant men and women serving our country in the Armed Forces. There's an old saying: Home is where your heart is. Funny how a heart can travel halfway around the world and still be home—just one thought away.

And for Chambrey—my Ivy.

Acknowledgments

There are so many elements combined to bring a book to life. I certainly couldn't do it on my own. I owe a huge thank you to my publisher, Cedar Fort, Inc. for always believing in me, and my stories.

I owe a huge thank you to Brandi Carroll, counselor at Cedar Valley Elementary School in Killeen, TX, for her insight into the process of Deployment and Reunion.

Thanks to my many friends and colleagues who have helped in the critique process—Erin Klingler, Josi Kilpack, Millie Martin, Deborah Frontiera, Bettina Williford, Mary Ann Hellinghausen, Jenny Suffredini, Ruth Baxter, Tim Crow, Barbara Holt and Pam Kinser. This book wouldn't be what it is without your input.

I'm grateful to be a part of LDStorymakers and SCBWI Houston—two wonderful organizations that not only support writers but foster friendship. After all, no one understands a writer better than another writer.

The best part about being an author—besides going to work in my pajamas—is visiting elementary schools and meeting so many awesome children. My greatest hope is to help cultivate their love of books and reading. *They* are the reason I write!

Most important, thank you to my family. I love you guys—you're the best!

1

Mud and Ivy

Mud sucks—seriously. With every step I took down Grandma's long driveway, I wondered if I'd be able to pull my shoe back out of the brown muck. Yuck! My six-year-old brother, Spencer, seemed to love our muddy morning walk to Edna Elementary School no matter how dirty his shoes got. But he'd convinced me long ago he was half pig—the kid has no manners at the table—so I guess I wasn't surprised.

Once we made it to the main road, I figured we were out of the danger zone. Wrong. We were out of the thick mud, but Spencer still managed to stomp through every puddle he could find.

"Your toes are going to turn into prunes," I hollered as Spencer jumped, both feet together, into a small pool of grayish-brown water that looked a little too much like Grandma's black bean soup. I didn't like to eat the stuff, and I really didn't want my little brother splashing it, or something that looked like it, all over my school clothes. We were only half a block from school, and the kid's shoes were as wet as our baby brother's diaper first thing in the morning. As he walked, all I could hear was *squish, squish, squish.*

"What's a prune?" Spencer asked.

"Something gross that Mom and Grandma eat. It keeps them normal, or regular, or sane, or something. I can't exactly remember."

Spencer laughed. "You think Mom and Grandma want to eat my feet?" He held up a dripping tennis shoe toward me, and I could imagine his shriveled-up, stinking toes wiggling inside. This thought— not to mention the disturbing image of Mom and Grandma nibbling on his toes—made me want to gag. Sometimes having a great imagination *isn't* such a great thing.

"You know what I think?" I replied. "I think you're going to make me late for school if you don't hurry up. Now come on." I started walking faster and didn't even look behind to see if Spencer was following. I could still hear his shoes squishing, and I almost felt sorry for his stubby first-grader legs trying to keep up.

As we reached the school, the bell sounded and every kid began to move a little faster. I turned to face Spencer, who was struggling to keep up. "Meet me at the flag pole," I reminded, like I'd done every day of school that year. Today would no doubt be another round of puddle-jumping. I was learning to keep my distance.

"Bye, Allie." Spencer waved and headed to the door at the far end of the building. I turned and started walking toward my class, the only sixth grade class at Edna Elementary.

If I still lived back in Killeen, Texas, I'd be in middle school by now—lockers, gym clothes, yearbooks, even cheerleading! But here I was, still with the little kids in elementary school. How fair is that?

But then I guess a lot of things in life can be unfair—like not being able to see your dad for a year because he's halfway around the world in Iraq doing his soldier duty. It would all soon be a memory, though. Dad would be coming home in May—only a month away. I could hardly wait!

When I walked into the classroom, my thoughts shifted. Something seemed to be different. What was it? Willy Simms was doing his usual how-annoying-can-I-be-today routine, this time filling up his cheeks with air and squishing his hands together on his face, making disgusting noises. Disturbing.

Celeste, Aubrey, and Tiffany, the popular girls, seemed to be huddled even tighter than usual. Those of us watching from the outside wished we knew what could be so funny for them to make all those giggles and gasps. The truth was, they were probably talking and laughing about the rest of us. It was easy to tell—point, look, giggle. Point, look, gasp. More giggles. Irritating!

Personally, I didn't want to know what they were gossiping about. But I *did* wonder what it would be like to have such close friends. The other kids in my class were nice to me, but it wasn't the same as having a really close friend. A best friend. Something I didn't have.

"Good morning, class." Mrs. Kaneko walked to the board at the front of the room and wrote the word *Ivy*. I wondered if we were going to start the day with a lesson on plants, but the thought didn't last long. "We have a new student." Mrs. Kaneko motioned her hand toward her desk, where a girl with short, blonde hair was sitting.

That was it! I knew something was different when I walked into the class. We had a new student, and hallelujah for that. I'd been "the new kid" for seven long months. I guess people don't often move to Edna, Idaho—go figure! Either way, I was just glad to give up the position.

"Ivy has moved here all the way from California." A new buzz erupted throughout the room. All eyes focused on the new girl, and her cheeks turned as red as one of Grandma's tomatoes. I could relate.

"Willy and Chase, will you two go get that empty desk against the back wall?" said Mrs. Kaneko. "Let's see, Ivy. Where should we have you sit?"

I quickly crossed my fingers and toes. *Please, please, please. Let her sit here!* I sat up tall in my desk and tried to make eye contact with my teacher. I even stuck my chin up and continued to mouth the words "please" in hopes that Mrs. Kaneko might be able to read lips.

When Mrs. Kaneko's eyes met mine, a smile spread across her always-pretty face. "Why don't we put you here with Allie, Matt, and Ben."

Yes! I let out a deep breath I hadn't realized I was holding.

Mine and Matt's desks were already facing each other, and Ben's desk joined ours to form a T. So Ben pulled his desk over next to Matt's, leaving a spot for the new girl's desk next to mine. I was suddenly in a very good mood—chocolate-chip-cookie good mood! Maybe now—finally—I'd have a really good friend at Edna Elementary. Maybe even a *best* friend.

As Ivy walked across the classroom to her new desk, Celeste whispered, "I heard that in California they have *Poison* Ivy."

Aubrey and Tiffany both tried to stifle their giggles. One even snorted.

I made no attempt to hide the glare aimed right at Celeste. It was no big secret that Celeste Holt was *not* my favorite person. I wondered why everyone else in the class acted like it would make their day to kiss her popular, stinkin' feet. She was big stuff around Edna Elementary. She was to Mrs. Kaneko's sixth grade class what a white Christmas is to most Americans—beautiful to look at, and most people really want it there for some reason. But cold and unpleasant if you're face to face with it for too long, especially if you're not wearing the right clothes, which I guess I never did. Whatever.

Mrs. Kaneko hadn't heard Celeste's comment. Figures. I could only hope Ivy hadn't either. I knew what it was like to start a new school. I'd done it three times in the past seven years, a fact of life when your dad's a soldier. It's not easy.

I hadn't realized how short Ivy was until I stood up to adjust our desks. She only came up to my ear, and I'm not what anyone would consider

tall. Just normal—regular—and thank goodness
for that because I didn't want to start eating prunes
anytime soon.

When Ivy looked at me, I could see something
very familiar in her face, or maybe it was in her eyes,
and yet I didn't even know her at all. It was a little
weird. And a little cool, like one of those déjà vu
things. My arms got goose bumps so I folded them.
I didn't want anyone to notice.

Matt asked her right off if she knew any movie
stars in California. Right.

"I'm from *northern* California," Ivy said. "Elk
Grove."

"Yeah?" Matt's eyebrows were raised, ready for
some big names. He obviously wanted to hear that
Orlando Bloom was her next-door neighbor and
Hillary Duff, her best friend.

I jumped in to help. "Movie stars live in *southern*
California." I only knew this because two years ago
we went to Disneyland in southern California, then
drove all the way up the coast to Oregon—a very
long drive. I hoped Ivy would be impressed with
how much I knew.

Matt shrugged. And Ben hadn't even looked
up from his workbook. We all went back to work,
but it was hard to concentrate with the thought
of making a good impression and possibly a best
friend swirling through my brain.

When Mrs. Kaneko announced morning recess, books were flung into desks. In less than sixty seconds the room cleared out, except for Ivy and me. I wanted to stick close to Ivy. I figured she needed me.

"Allie," asked Mrs. Kaneko, "why don't you show Ivy around the playground?"

"Sure," I replied. I was glad she'd asked. I was going to anyway, but this made it easier.

"So, how do you like Edna?" I asked as the two of us walked toward the playground.

Ivy shrugged. "It's okay, I guess. Small. Rainy. Muddy. At least today it is."

I wasn't sure if Ivy was trying to be funny, but I laughed. "Yeah. I know what you mean. I moved here from Texas last summer."

I looked over at Ivy, expecting her to say something. But her face looked like a blank page in a book. Nothing to say. We walked along in silence for a bit. The air was cool, and neither of us had grabbed our jackets.

What the heck, I thought. I'll keep *myself* company. "We're living here with my grandma while my dad's in Iraq," I said. "He's a soldier."

Again, I looked at Ivy. Waited. The girl must have something to say. But she kept looking out at the empty potato field behind the school. What could be so interesting about those stupid rows of dirt?

Maybe this friend-making stuff was a mistake.

When Ivy finally spoke, her voice was soft. "How long has your dad been gone?"

"Too long," I replied. How long had it been anyway? It felt like a million years. but I decided to figure it out. "I guess it's been eleven months because he's coming home next month."

"Do you miss him?" she asked.

This surprised me a little. Whenever I told anyone that my dad was a soldier and in Iraq, it seemed like they never wanted to talk about it. Probably because on the news they always show pictures of Iraq that are kind of scary. At least to me. Sometimes I wondered if Dad was ever scared.

"I miss him a lot." I could feel my throat starting to ache, like when I'm going to cry. That was the *last* thing I needed to happen. I took a deep breath and blinked a few times.

For the first time, Ivy looked at me, and I felt embarrassed. "I got some dust in my eye," I said, which was totally lame, and totally a lie. It had been raining for three days. Any dust in Edna had turned into a mud puddle of Grandma's black bean soup a few days ago, just waiting for my brother to splash in it.

"Don't worry," said Ivy. "I have that problem all the time." I'm not positive, but I don't think Ivy was talking about dust.

A familiar ringing of girls' laughter reached my ears. We both turned our heads at the same time. There was Celeste, standing with her arms folded and looking like she'd just taken a sip of sour milk. Aubrey and Tiffany stood on each side of her like a pair of bookends. Made me wonder if the girl could actually stand on her own. With her eyes still fixed on us, Celeste tilted her head and whispered something that brought on another round of giggles from the bookends.

Ivy shifted her eyes down to the ground, then back to that field. I wasn't sure what she was looking for, but I had a feeling it wasn't an empty potato field.

I raised my chin and glared into that face—the one that some call pretty—for as long as I could stand it. Then I nudged Ivy's shoulder with mine.

"Hey, c'mon. Let me show you around."

Ivy was still looking away and I barely heard her say, "Okay."

I couldn't resist glancing back one last time at Celeste and her friends. But the three had turned their attention to a group of seventh grade boys playing baseball in the junior high school's field across the street. Typical!

Maybe I'd been spending too much time around my little brother because at that moment I did what every kid wants to do when they're really mad at someone—I stuck out my tongue. I did. And it was pointing at Celeste Holt and her dumb bookend friends.

Before I even had a chance to consider how stupid and babyish I was looking, I heard another laugh, this time a beautiful laugh.

It came from Ivy.

2

What the Cat Coughed Up

"Well, look what the cat coughed up!" Grandma was the queen of weird sayings. After a year of living in her one-hundred-year-old yellow house, I was used to it. Spencer and I had just wandered through the front door after a long day of school followed by a watery walk home. The rain fell on and off all day, and unfortunately for us, when school let out, it was off again. If it had been on, Mom or Grandma would've taken pity and picked us up.

Spencer responded with a long "meee-ow." Not only was my little brother crazy about animals—always pretending to be one—but he just didn't understand Grandma and her sayings the way I did.

"Take those soggy shoes off, Mr. Cat," said Grandma. "I don't want mud traipsed all through my house."

Spencer meowed again as he sat down next to the door and untied his shoelaces. I knew a dangerous situation when I saw it. I quickly kicked off my tennis shoes and made my way toward the living room in search of Mom. I wanted to tell her about my day.

"Mom, I'm home." I'd sung these exact same words, this exact same way every school day since I was five. Mom usually greeted me with a "Hey, kiddo" or "How was your day, sweetie?" But today there was no response. I knew Mom was home because The Bruise—that's what we call our mini-van because it's sort of purplish-reddish—was parked outside.

"I think she's in her room," Grandma said from the kitchen.

Mom's door was closed, and I figured she might be trying to get my baby brother, Tommy, to sleep, so I quietly opened the door and tiptoed in. Tommy was asleep in his crib, so it was a good thing I didn't knock. And Mom looked like she was asleep on her bed too. That was unusual for this time of day.

I was about to leave when Mom rolled over. Her eyes were puffy and red. I knew this look—she'd been crying.

A sense of panic came crashing through my body. "What's wrong?" I should have whispered since Tommy was asleep, but my mouth didn't want to.

Mom brought one finger to her lips to shush me, then motioned to come close. I walked quietly and quickly to the bed, and sat down next to her.

"I got a call from Daddy today." Mom's voice was soft, but sounded a little flat. Like she didn't have any feelings left inside. From the looks of her eyes, I had to wonder if she'd cried them all out.

"What did he say?" My heart was thumping around in my body. "Is he okay?"

"Yes, yes, yes . . . he's fine." As Mom hugged me, my heart thumping began to settle down. "But he's not coming home next month."

I squirmed away from Mom's embrace and looked into those red, puffy eyes. "But he's been gone almost a year. It's his turn to come home."

My face felt hot. I wanted to scream.

Mom could tell because she tried to pull me back into the hug. But I didn't want one. I wanted Dad back home. That's all. I stood up and started to leave, but Mom grabbed my hand.

"I know you're disappointed. I am too."

I didn't want to talk about it. Didn't want to hear excuses. But Mom kept a hold of my hand. I hated when she did that. I felt like a dog on a leash who wanted to run.

"It's only two extra months. He'll be back the end of July.

"Mom!" I raised my voice, and Mom raised her shushing finger. "We're going to the Grand Canyon in June, remember?"

"We'll still go—maybe August." Mom looked like she was trying to convince herself. I wasn't so sure. "They asked Dad's battalion to stay another two months. But the minute he gets back, we're heading to Killeen and then to the Grand Canyon."

I jerked my hand loose. "It's not fair."

Without closing Mom's door, I left. I didn't stop for Grandma's treats or even to use the bathroom. I just ran up those stupid green stairs like I'd done every day for a stupid year and threw my face into my stupid pillow.

Stupid, stupid.

Stupid!

Back in Killeen, I'd been to the beauty shop once, on my tenth birthday. Cindy, the lady who cut my hair, first gave it a shampoo. Her long fingernails combed through my hair, and I thought I'd fall asleep right there in her chair.

I could still feel those fingernails combing through my hair as I pulled my eyelids open. But instead of Cindy and her fingernails, it was Mom. When had she grown her fingernails out? I hadn't noticed.

The sun was low in the sky, leaving shadows on the far wall.

"You feeling any better?" she asked.

I shrugged. It was all coming back, and a part of me wanted to roll over and return to my beauty shop dream.

"Daddy asked how you were doing. He said he has a surprise for you."

This almost made me want to ask, "What?" but I didn't.

Mom's fingers continued to comb my hair. "He'll give it to you as soon as he gets back."

I guess Mom decided to change the subject. "So how was your day today?" This simple question made me remember that aside from Dad's bad news, today had been an okay day.

I rubbed my face and sat up. "I have a new friend . . . I think."

"Really?" Mom's eyes grew wide. That meant "tell me more."

I stretched and spoke through a yawn. "She's really short. Nice, I guess. And she's from California."

"What's her name?"

"Ivy." It was an easy name to remember.

"I like that name," Mom said.

"It's okay," I said. I was trying not to get my hopes up. Even though I wanted Ivy to be my friend, even my best friend, she was so quiet. It seemed a little weird.

"Maybe you can invite her over sometime," Mom said.

I hadn't thought of that. "Maybe."

Mom wouldn't quit. "Her mom can call me, if she has any questions."

It sounded like a good plan. But would Ivy want to come? I hoped she would.

I turned to Mom. "Do you think I should invite her over on Friday, after school?" Why waste time, I thought. I'd already been best-friendless for eleven months in this hick town. I might as well make the best of my last three.

From the smile on Mom's face, I knew she understood.

"Sure, why not?"

For the rest of the afternoon, the house was quieter than usual. Grandma and Mom didn't even watch the evening news—something they *always* did, but only when Spencer and I were out of the room. If we came back in, they always turned it off. I wondered why.

When Mom told Spencer about Dad, he cried a big bawl-baby cry. I showed him on the calendar that two months wasn't all that long. I don't think he believed me.

I don't think I believed myself.

After dinner, Grandma asked Spencer and me to take out the chicken scraps—a somewhat disgusting chore considering that every leftover piece of food from the entire day was piled into the same bucket—leftover oatmeal, a half-eaten pickle, potato peelings, you name it. Not only did it look gross, but sometimes it smelled worse. I thought it was a little weird, though, that Grandma wanted Spencer to come with me since he was still afraid of Grandma's crazy goat named Abraham Lincoln— who thought he was a watch dog and loved to chase little kids—but maybe she figured I'd protect him. I guess that all depended on my mood. After all, it was kinda funny watching him squeal.

Spencer was just glad to be doing something with me. This fact alone *almost* made me feel guilty for what I was about to put him through with Abe. I wouldn't let it get too out of hand—just a good chase ending with me running out to save the day (and Spencer's rear end from making contact with Abe's horns).

As Spencer and I headed out the kitchen door that opened to the side yard of the big yellow house and made it halfway to the gate leading to the field where the chicken coop was, I glanced back to the house. I hoped no one was watching. The last thing I needed was to get into trouble from Mom or Grandma. Then I wouldn't be able to have Ivy come over on Friday.

It was a good thing I checked, because both Mom and Grandma were standing outside, next to the kitchen door. Did they sense that I was up to no good? Sometimes with Grandma and Mom, I had to wonder if they could read minds. Instead of sending Spencer out to the chicken coop alone to face Abe, I grabbed the bucket from him and placed one arm around his shoulder. He squirmed away, but I could only hope that Grandma and Mom noticed my sisterly gesture.

The sun had almost completely gone down, but there was still a little grey daylight left. As I opened the gate, I motioned for my little brother to enter. "C'mon, let's get this done already. I've got more important things to do."

Spencer stood outside the gate and wouldn't move. "You first," he said.

I wanted to grab the little dork by his shirtsleeve and toss him in, but another glance back confirmed the fact that we still had an audience at the kitchen door. What the heck were they doing anyway? I swear, I'll never figure out those two. And the creepy thing was, I had a feeling that these things were contagious, or hereditary or something like that. Grandma always said, "It's in the genes, Allie." When I was little, I'd always look down at my pants, and then shrug. I just didn't get it!

"Come on, Dweebazoid. Follow me," I said with a huff as I walked through the gate. I knew Mom and Grandma couldn't hear all the way out here. I held the gate open long enough for him to get through, but let it slam shut on his backside. The force of the gate pushed him forward just a bit, but he regained his balance and continued to follow me without a yelp, or yowl, or a "why'd ya do that?" I wasn't getting any big-sisterly satisfaction this evening at all. Aside from Ivy, the day had been a total bust.

About five steps into the field, Spencer yanked hard on the back of my shirt. I was almost thrown off balance. Was the kid trying to get back at me for the years of torment? Why would it start bothering him now? Besides, he'd have his chance with Tommy in a few years—not that I'd let him lay a stubby little finger on our baby brother.

"There's something moving out there," Spencer whispered.

"Duh."

"Don't ya see it?" he squeaked.

"It's Abe. And if you're going to be such a baby, why don't you go back to the house. Mom and Grandma are waiting near the kitchen door for you anyway. Guess they figured you'd be too chicken to feed the chickens." I let out a little snort of a laugh, pleased with my play on words.

"There's something *else* out there. On the other side of Abe. It's smaller. Maybe a coyote. Jesse Tucker told me that out on their ranch a coyote killed some sheep. His dad tried to shoot it with his rifle but it got away."

"Shut up," I said, but in my mind I was wondering if coyotes ate children. I also didn't take another step forward. It probably wasn't a coyote. The Tuckers lived at least fifteen miles out of town. Grandma's house was *in* town . . . barely. Actually, it was right on the edge of town. On the same road that led out to the Tucker's ranch.

After giving my head a slight tilt and squinting my eyes, I could see it! The possible-coyote. And it was standing behind Abe. But if it was a coyote, wouldn't it be trying to eat Abe for dinner already? And wouldn't Abe be acting a little freaked out or something? I know I would, if a coyote was trying to nibble on me.

But no. Abe was standing there all protectively—like he always was with those silly chickens. Just when I was seriously considering the idea of turning back around and flushing the scraps down the toilet, the possible-coyote began to walk around the backside of Abe.

I couldn't believe my eyes.

3

Standing Upwind

"Now don't go gettin' your hopes up too high. We'll do our best, and that's all we can do."

"He's soooo cute," I said, as I stroked the back of the baby goat's neck.

"Yes, he is. But he's awful weak right now. His momma died giving birth to him, and none of the other nanny goats will adopt him. He's taken to the bottle fairly well and seems to be doing better."

Grandma stroked the baby goat's neck as she spoke.

"Is he going to die without his mommy?" Spencer asked, lip quivering.

"I hope not, sweetie. Mrs. Miller felt like he'd have the best chance of surviving if he had the companionship of another goat. To be honest, I wasn't sure Old Abe was up to the task. He can be pretty ornery at times . . . "

Spencer and I looked at each other. We both knew firsthand about the orneriness of Abe Lincoln.

"But surprisingly, Abe has taken to the little thing. He's already acting very protective." Grandma smiled. "Isn't that sweeter than baby's breath?"

We both nodded, but I didn't remember Tommy having sweet breath at all. As I held up my hand to tickle the baby goat's chin, he began to suck on two of my fingers.

"I think he's hungry," Grandma said.

"Can I feed him?" I asked.

"I think you'd better if you want to keep those fingers," Grandma said with a laugh. Spencer gasped.

"What are we going to call him?" Spencer asked.

"I don't know," Grandma replied. "Got any good ideas?"

"How about Brownie?" Spencer was looking all proud like he'd thought up the best name in the universe.

I rolled my eyes and let out a sort of puffing sound. "Just because he has brown hair doesn't mean we should call him Brownie. How original."

"Allison." That was all Mom said, and she didn't need to say more—I recognized the tone. Mom had been standing next to Grandma the whole time, but she was holding Tommy.

"I don't want to name him Brownie because he's brown," Spencer said. "I want to name him Brownie because brownies are my favorite dessert." He looked pleased with himself.

"Well, chewy chocolate chip cookies are my favorite desert, but you don't see me wanting to call him Chocolate Chip . . . or Chewy."

For some reason this made Spencer laugh—not the reaction I was shooting for. Grandma laughed too, but when she finished, she said, "Why don't we take it to bed and hope we don't squish it in the middle of the night." Another one of Grandma's famous sayings. Grandma thought we should take every decision to bed. Spencer looked at Grandma with a puzzled expression, and I just shook my head.

The next day at school I was both excited and nervous to see Ivy again. I wanted to tell her about the baby goat and how we first thought it was a coyote about to kill our Grandma's other goat like the one at the Tuckers. But would she even care?

I also wanted to tell her about Dad and how he couldn't come home till July—two extra months. Even though I'd only known Ivy for a day, something told me she'd understand why this made me mad. And if she could, I knew she'd be my friend. As for best friend—I was trying not to wish too hard.

I kept a steady pace as my brother and I headed toward the school. Thank goodness the puddles had almost disappeared, or were a whole lot smaller. I think Spencer even managed to make it to school with dry shoes. Progress.

Because I'd walked at a record pace, we made it to school earlier than usual. Only one of the buses had arrived, and I don't think all of the teachers were even there yet. Maybe I'd been in too much of a hurry. But Grandma always says, "The first one in line gets to stand upwind." I knew this couldn't be true, but it made me want to be early for some reason.

"Meet me at the flagpole," I hollered to Spencer as usual before heading around to the back of the school and the playground. Even though I was in the sixth grade, I had to admit, I loved playing on the playground. At least the swings. My favorite thing was to swing as high as I could, then close my eyes and lean my head back. It made me a little dizzy, and sometimes I thought I might fall right out of the swing, but there was also a feeling that swept through my entire body—like I was flying, or maybe floating through the air. And it didn't matter if it was on the swings at Kennedy Elementary in Texas or Edna Elementary in Idaho, or even on Mars. I was in my own world. In my own time.

Lately, if I closed my eyes tight enough, and flew back and forth long enough, I could imagine my dad swinging right next to me. We were flying together. Flying free. No rules, no boundaries, no million miles between us. My heart imagined all the air space between us just disappeared. We were together again.

It always worked . . . until I opened my eyes.

As I rounded the corner of the school and glanced to the swings, goose bumps rose up on my arms. I didn't even need to squint. I knew exactly who the smallish girl with short blonde hair, swinging back and forth, was.

I wanted to run, but didn't want to seem anxious, so I forced my feet to take their time getting me over to the swing set.

"Hey," I said as my shoes crunched across small pebbles.

My possible-friend looked in my direction and nodded. I think she even smiled, but just a little.

I dropped my backpack from my shoulder and it fell to the ground. "You're here early."

"You too," Ivy replied.

She wasn't saying much, so I figured I would. "I like to swing." I hopped onto the plastic black seat hanging from thick metal links. "At recess, everyone hogs the swings. So if you want your chance, you have to come before school starts."

This was only a theory. It made sense though, and explained why I was at school so early. I don't know why I wanted an excuse for this, but I did.

"So why are you here early?" I asked.

Ivy slowed down until she was barely swinging. I wondered if maybe she'd stand up and walk off, but instead, she started to talk.

"Today's my mom's first day of work."

"Did she drop you off early?"

Ivy chewed on her lip for a minute, like she was thinking real hard. "Actually, she got a job here at the school, in the cafeteria." Now she was staring at her feet.

"I like cafeteria food." I wasn't sure why I said that; it just came out. I hate when my mouth works before my brain.

Ivy looked up at me. "Serious?"

I shrugged. "It's okay." Great! Now I sounded like a total dorkwad, but Ivy smiled.

"Do you like to swing high?" she asked.

A huge grin pulled up the corners of my mouth. "Race you to the top."

"Beat you there."

● ● ● ● ●

Dear Dad,

I have a new friend. Probably the best friend I've had since we moved to Edna. Her name is Ivy and she's from northern California, so she doesn't know any movie stars but in her old school she met the governor. He used to be a movie star and now he's a governor. I think either one would be a cool job.

Ivy loves to swing and so do I. Something in my heart—or maybe it's in my genes—tells me that when you were a kid, you liked to swing too. I bet you still do. I think about you when I'm swinging.

I wish you didn't have to stay longer in Iraq, but I guess we'll survive until July. I really miss you. Come home soon so we can swing together.

Love, Allie

4

Two Beans in a Burrito

As the week went on, it became freakishly amazing how much Ivy and I had in common. Not only did we both like to swing, but we both loved chocolate chip cookies (the chewy, gooey kind), ramen noodles (especially chicken flavor), creamy peanut butter, and anything Harry Potter. We also agreed that the books are better, but Harry is *way* hotter in the movies. The book covers don't come close.

Grandma said we were two beans in a burrito. Mom called us kindred spirits. She knew all about this since she had one—Trudy Pickett, her best friend since kindergarten. I was just glad that the both of them got over the fact that I'd never end up as a kindred spirit or a bean in a burrito with Trudy's daughter, Penny Pickett. Not only was she too young for me to hang out with, but she had a big mouth and *never* stopped talking. Ivy was a good listener—one more thing we had in common.

"What's your favorite breakfast food?" I asked Ivy as we sat down next to each other at one end of a long table. The cafeteria was humming as usual with every student from fourth to sixth grade.

"Hmmmm." Ivy was thinking hard about my question. I could tell because her eyebrows scrunched together. Then, they shot up and her eyes got big. "I know. Doughnuts."

"Your mom lets you eat doughnuts for breakfast?"

Ivy grinned. "No, but my dad does sometimes. When it's his weekend."

"His weekend for what—fixing breakfast? Whenever my dad cooks, it's pancakes or nothing."

I smiled, thinking about Dad and his yummy pancakes with maple syrup, but at the same time, Ivy's grin faded. "It's sort of like that. Or it used to be anyway."

Now I was really confused. "What do you mean?"

"My mom and dad are divorced." Ivy poked her fork into a green bean and stuck it into her mouth. "Back in Elk Grove I'd spend every other weekend with my dad—but I'm not sure how it's supposed to work since we're in Edna now." Ivy poked her fork into another green bean, only this time she didn't stick it into her mouth, just tapped it on her tray like a little hammer.

I didn't really know what to say to that, so I nodded like I understood. I suppose in a way I did. Even though my parents weren't divorced, Dad was far away in Iraq. I understood what it was like to be far away from someone I loved.

Ivy tapped that poor, overcooked green bean until it was a pile of mush, fit for nothing but a baby. Instead of eating it, she eased her fork out of the green glob, plunged it into her spaghetti, and began to spin it around. "I miss my dad."

"I hear ya."

"Sometime this summer I'll be seeing him again. I just don't know when, exactly. Mom says it's being discussed . . . which isn't such a great thing because my mom and dad don't discuss anything without arguing—especially about me and Ty."

"That totally stinks."

My words came out a little louder than I really wanted them to and I looked around, a little self-conscious.

Celeste Holt, my not-so-favorite person, and her followers happened to be sitting at the end of the table next to ours, and they had obviously overheard my little outburst. Celeste leaned toward Tiffany but didn't bother to speak softly.

"Doesn't she know a bath will take care of that?"

Tiffany and Aubrey laughed. Did those two even have any brains of their own? Obviously not, the way they followed Celeste around like lost little puppy dogs just waiting for a pat on the head. Pathetic!

My body stiffened with each annoying giggle. I was fed up with these three—especially Celeste and her need be princess of the universe. If this was what being popular turned people into, I'd rather be a nobody the rest of my life.

"Why are some people such jerks?" I was looking at Ivy as I spoke, but my comment was actually meant for other ears—pathetic, popular princess ears. And her stupid puppy dogs.

Ivy spoke in a softer tone. "Are they always like this?"

My eyes glanced toward the obnoxious trio, then back to Ivy. "Unfortunately, yes. All they think about is clothes, hair, boys, and of course, putting other people down. I don't know why Mrs. Kaneko even lets them sit together in class."

"Maybe for the same reason she lets us sit together. And Matt and Ben."

I took a deep breath in an attempt to calm down. "I don't know. Maybe you're right."

Ivy sat up straight on the bench and tried to keep a serious face. "I'm always right." That was it—we both laughed, and it felt good.

As kids started to leave the cafeteria and Ivy and I slurped up the last of our chocolate milk through straws, a woman dressed in a familiar light blue cafeteria-lady uniform, complete with white apron and hair net, walked up behind Ivy, placed her hands on her shoulders, and then lowered her body down for a brief hug from behind.

"How's my girl doing?"

"Hi, Mom."

Even in her cafeteria uniform—hair net and all—Mrs. Peterson was pretty. Not a flashy, movie-star kind of pretty. (How flashy can you be in a cafeteria uniform and hair net anyway?) She had a natural type of beauty, without wearing makeup.

She didn't need to. "And this must be Allie. I've heard so much about you."

"Hi." I waved with my fork in my hand and spoke with a mouth full of spaghetti. I couldn't help it. I'd just taken a bite. Still, I thought of Grandma. I could hear her voice as clear as if she was standing next to Mrs. Peterson. *Allie, the barn's out back if you can't find your manners.*

"Hey, sweetie. I have to stay late today. Hopefully only an hour or so. Paperwork." Mrs. Peterson gave a big sigh, then held out her hand. "Here's the key. When you meet up with Ty to walk home, ask him to throw pot pies into the oven at 4:15, okay? You can make a salad."

Ivy nodded. "Okay."

"It was nice to finally meet you, Allie." Mrs. Peterson gave her daughter's shoulders another squeeze. "See you later."

"Bye," we said together.

After Mrs. Peterson passed through the kitchen door, a burst of laughter erupted from Celeste and her stupid puppy dog friends. It sounded like they'd been holding their breath for a million years, and finally exploded in hysterical giggles.

Then came the words—ugly words, slicing their way slow and on purpose through the thick cafeteria air like knives heading straight toward Ivy.

"See you later, sweetie."

"Bye-bye, Mommy."

Their voices were sickeningly sweet.

Next in disgust, "How embarrassing." "I'd rather die than have my mom be a *cafeteria* lady."

The giggles started up again, and there was only one thing certain in my mind. No matter what the cost, I was going stop them.

Without realizing my body was in motion, I found myself standing at the end of Celeste's table. My heart pounded as words spit from my lips. "You got a problem?"

Celeste stood to face me, and for the first time I realized we were exactly the same size. To be honest, she'd always seemed taller, bigger. Maybe it was her ego.

Our eyes met straight across from each other. Celeste gave a half huff, half laugh before she spoke. "No. But it looks like you do." She looked pleased with herself as her eyes darted back to the puppy dogs. As if on cue, they both forced a laugh.

"You know what? I *do* have a problem—"

"Um . . . yeah. I think we already knew that."

Celeste put her hands on her hips, and when she spoke, her head bobbed side to side, accentuating every syllable. She looked ridiculous. I wanted to give her a *real* reason to bob her head.

The two of us stood there in the Edna Elementary cafeteria, our eyes burning holes into each other. The large, always noisy room was still. Even though my voice was steady—almost calm—the surrounding silence made my words sound loud.

"I'm only going to say this once. Leave. Ivy. Alone. Got that?"

Celeste's eyes turned to ice crystals, and her voiced matched. "Oh, I'm scared. Scared of Allie Claybrook. What ya gonna do? Get your Dad to come home from Iraq and shoot me?"

Celeste might as well have punched me in the stomach; her words hurt that much. "You leave my dad out of this. You don't know anything about him so just shut up!" My dad was the bravest man I knew. He was my hero, and I didn't want to hear her say stupid things about him. She didn't know anything!

I could start to feel my eyes stinging, but I was *not* going to bawl in front of Celeste Holt. I'd *never* give her the satisfaction. Thanks to Mrs. Barker, the head cafeteria lady, I wouldn't have to. Her large body moved with amazing speed toward us. The stern expression on her face matched her voice.

"What's going on here?"

Celeste plastered on her sticky-sweet smile and shrugged. "I have no idea." It wasn't much of a stretch for the girl to play stupid.

"We're fine," I lied.

"Good. Then the two of you shake hands and make up."

Celeste turned what appeared to be sincere eyes toward Mrs. Baker—but every kid in the sixth grade knew better. "I will, if she will." No wonder Celeste had all the teachers fooled, thinking she was as sweet as honey. Actually, she was more of a honeybee, waiting to sting some poor innocent victim. The girl was such a fake. I bet she could fool anyone over twenty.

I couldn't even respond. I just stood there hoping she didn't notice how I was trembling, and on the verge of tears. Once again, I told myself—I am *not* going to cry!

Mrs. Barker's round arms were barely folded in front of her, and she looked at me all impatient, like this whole thing was my fault.

Just when I thought I might fall apart, a soft voice came from directly behind me. I knew that voice—Ivy. I turned my entire body around to face her, and there she was. But something in her expression seemed out of place. I'd expected her to look more distraught—sympathetic. After all, I was practically defending her honor. Or something close to it, I think. Actually, I was starting to feel very confused about everything.

"It's okay," Ivy said with too much calmness. But her eyes were speaking to me, though I wasn't sure

I understood the language. If Mom was right, and we truly were kindred spirits, this was definitely the test to prove it.

With my back still to Mrs. Barker and Celeste, Ivy slowly took each of my hands in hers and slightly shook them up and down as she spoke. She repeated herself. "It's okay, Allie. I think you should shake her hand."

Only Ivy would see my smile—and only briefly as I realized that within her left hand, and my right, a transfer had taken place—a transfer of something smooshy and gooey . . . and wonderful. My mind flashed back to the gooey pile of green bean mush that, moments earlier, had been sitting in Ivy's tray, pounded to a pulp. Now it was in my right hand. My hand-shaking hand.

"Isn't that sweet," Tiffany said with fake enthusiasm.

Aubrey snorted. Seriously—she snorted.

I quickly turned around to see Celeste shoot a scolding glance to Aubrey who had just embarrassed herself, therefore embarrassing Celeste. I almost felt sorry for Aubrey as she shrank down into the bench.

Celeste returned to character before Mrs. Barker caught on.

"Well?" Mrs. Barker tapped her fingers against her arm.

Holding Celeste's gaze, I raised my right hand to meet hers. When our fingertips connected, I grabbed Celeste's hand in a firm, vigorous handshake, that aside from the green-goo involved, my dad would be proud of. (Dad always gave firm handshakes, but I doubted his ever involved anything green and slimy.)

As expected, Celeste yanked her hand out of my firm grasp only to discover something green and slimy oozing between her fingers and dripping down her palm. Her scream echoed through the cafeteria, which was now filled with laughter from everyone except the puppy dogs.

And just to creep Celeste out a little more, I gave an exaggerated sniff and wiggled my nose in the process. I'd leave the rest up to her imagination.

5

The Green Bean Handshake

"I'm surprised by this, Allie." Mrs. Kaneko stood with her arms folded, wearing that same disappointed face Mom was so good at—the one that let you know you'd messed up big time.

I hated that look.

"She started it," I said, shooting a stare to

Celeste, who was imitating Mrs. Kaneko, only more dramatic with her hip popped out and one foot tapping. Did she seriously think I was scared of her? Mrs. Kaneko—maybe. My mom—most definitely. Grandma—always. Celeste Holt—never!

Celeste huffed as she folded her arms in front of her perfectly matching outfit. Then she let out a whine.

"She smeared green snot all over me."

"Your hand," I corrected, then looked down at my tennis shoes. I didn't want her to see me smile right then. It would only make me look guilty.

But my face couldn't help it. If for no other reason, I was happy that Celeste thought the mooshed green bean was something even more disgusting than it really was. This made any trouble I was about to be in totally worth it. Still, I needed to defend myself.

"She was making fun of Ivy's mom, who works in the cafeteria." I almost didn't want to bring up the next issue, but honestly, it was what sent me all ballistic. "And she said something about my dad. About him coming home from Iraq." There was a slight pause before I could finish my sentence. "And shooting her."

Mrs. Kaneko stood in silence for a long time, shaking her head back and forth. When she finally spoke, her voice was calm.

"I'm very disappointed in both of you."

Celeste huffed again, but Mrs. Kaneko didn't seem to notice. Instead she motioned with her hand. "Follow me."

After a silent walk down the hall of Edna Elementary with only the *click, click* of Mrs. Kaneko's shoes, the three of us entered our classroom. It was still empty since everyone was at recess—something we'd missed. I was still feeling too much satisfaction that Celeste thought the green bean was snot to regret it. The thought was so disgusting; I'd have probably lost my cookies if it had been me who received the green bean handshake.

"Allie, you grab your desk. Celeste, grab yours. You two will be sitting together for the next month." Mrs. Kaneko's voice sounded pleasant as usual. As if she were saying, "Allie, you erase the board and Celeste, you water the plant." But she might as well have said, "Allie, go sit next to that creature over there—the one that's part skunk, part grizzly bear, and part rattlesnake."

"Mrs. Kaneko—" Celeste whined.

I joined in. "Till school gets out?"

"Yep," she said. "Over here, ladies. On the other side of my desk."

It was obvious by her expression that no amount of whining or complaining would change

Mrs. Kaneko's mind. As I dragged my desk away from Ivy's, I finally began to regret my decision. Maybe it hadn't been such a good one after all.

Celeste continued to make noises each time she exhaled—could someone please teach the girl to breathe quietly? I wanted to say something like, *can you breathe to yourself?*, but I didn't want to get any further on Mrs. Kaneko's bad side.

A thought occurred to me. Maybe some logical reasoning would change Mrs. Kaneko's mind. "Ivy and I only sat together for three days. She doesn't know anyone else in the class."

"Then I guess this will give her the opportunity to get to know the others better."

Celeste went next. "I won't. No way. I refuse to sit with *her.*" She said "her" as if it meant a disgusting pile of sewage.

"Then I guess you'll have to sit with Mr. Barnes in the principal's office until you change your mind."

As Celeste and I moved our desks across from each other, the rest of the sixth grade wandered in from lunch recess. Cheeks were red, bangs were sweaty, and jackets and sweaters were tied around waists. I'd just missed a perfect spring afternoon recess. Figures.

It didn't take long for everyone to notice the change. And when Mrs. Kaneko confirmed to the class that Celeste and I would be sitting together for the remaining month of school, I wanted to throw up.

Ivy looked totally bummed sitting across the room with Ben and Matt. Tiffany looked like she was about to bawl. Aubrey looked lost. And Celeste looked like she wanted to rip off my head with those fangs of hers and swallow it whole.

This day was not turning out well. At all.

The last few hours of school passed incredibly slow. I wondered how I could possibly survive four more weeks staring into the sour-milk face of Celeste Holt for seven hours a day. If Mrs. Kaneko was trying to teach the class a lesson on torture, she couldn't have picked a better way.

At least now Celeste was doing her best to ignore me. When we colored our maps of South America, she leaned forward, using her long blonde hair as a curtain hanging between us. And I was fine with that. The less I was forced to look at that face, the better.

As I put the finishing touches on Chile—I'd colored it green in memory of the smooshed green bean that had landed me in exile with Celeste—a folded piece of paper landed right in the middle of Brazil—purple, by the way. I looked around and noticed Ivy at the pencil sharpener a few feet away.

After covering the piece of paper with my hand, I quickly slid it past Paraguay and Uruguay and down the coast of Argentina until it landed in my lap. A quick glance across the room confirmed that Mrs. Kaneko was busy. I unfolded the paper and read.

Allie,

Meet me after school and we can walk part of the way home together. I'm really sorry you have to sit with Celeste.

Your friend,
Ivy

P.S. Did you see her face when you shook her hand? Total freak out!

I was about to turn to Ivy and wave or something, but Celeste's words changed my plans.

"What's that—a love letter?" Celeste's was in her usual cranky mood, and I was shocked she was even speaking to me. She was curious, though. I know better than anyone what curiosity makes people do. I was determined to give her something to be cranky—as well as curious—about.

"Maybe," I replied.

Celeste gave a humorless laughed. "Right."

I shrugged and stuck the folded letter in my pocket. But not before I noticed Celeste's eyebrow raise ever so slightly. I'd piqued her interest. And even though she didn't want to let on, I knew I had something good going on here and I could totally mess with Celeste's mind. I couldn't wait to tell Ivy.

An hour later, when the school bell rang, I made a dash toward Ivy. Finally, I was free from my "jail time" with Celeste.

Ivy looked relieved to see me. The first words out of her mouth were, "Are you mad at me?"

"Are you serious? You're my new hero—well, next to my dad. The green bean handshake was totally worth five weeks of exile with Celeste—I think." We both laughed, slung our backpacks over our shoulders, and headed toward the door.

"My mom usually drives us," Ivy said, "but today we're walking."

"We?"

"My brother and I."

"I have to walk with my brother every day . . . unfortunately."

I'd become somewhat of an expert on brothers—I had two now. Tommy wasn't so bad. As a matter of fact, at four months old, he was a little round ball of cuteness. But Spencer—that was another story altogether.

We walked outside and I pointed to the flagpole. "There he is now."

"He's so cute." Ivy's voice went all high and squeaky like she'd just seen a fluffy white bunny.

As if he knew what I was thinking, Spencer started hopping up and down, and waving his hands. "Hi, Allie!"

I stuck my hands in my sweatshirt pockets and tilted my head to the side. "Come on."

Spencer turned to Ivy. "Who are you?"

"She's my friend," I said.

"I'm Ivy."

"Cool," Spencer said, and I wasn't sure why.

Ivy pointed across the street to the junior high. "And there's my brother over there—Ty."

"He's wearing a tie?" Spencer asked.

Ivy laughed. "His name is Ty. See him across the street? He's wearing a green t-shirt."

Now I don't know why I hadn't put two and two together about Ivy's brother. But as we walked toward the guy with the green t-shirt—the guy who was looking more and more like a hottie with each step toward the junior high—the pieces began to come together. Why did I think she had a *younger* brother? She's said something about him liking baseball earlier. This automatically sent images of Spencer wearing Dad's black baseball cap and begging me to play catch with him into my brain. But Ivy's brother was definitely not in the little dweebazoid category that Spencer belonged to. Not at all.

As we approached Ivy's brother, I couldn't help but notice a few similarities between the two—blond hair and blue eyes were the most obvious. But where Ivy's hair was short (for a girl) and straight, Ty's was a little longer than most of the Edna boys, and a little messy looking like the wind blew through it. He was also more tan than Ivy. To be honest, if someone placed him in a lineup of guys and asked me to pick out the one from California, I'd choose him.

"Where's Mom?" Ty asked when we were only halfway across the street dividing the elementary school from the junior high.

"She had to work late so we're walking."

Ty hefted his backpack from where it rested on the sidewalk and slung it over his shoulder.

He looked from his sister, to me, then back to his sister. "Is this Allie?"

My cheeks felt hot. How did he know my name?

"Yep." Then Ivy motioned to my little brother. "And this is Spencer."

Ty looked at me and gave a slight nod. "Hey."

I wanted to say something mature, or at least cool. But my brain froze. "Hi," I squeaked.

The four of us headed down the sidewalk toward Main Street. Ty led the way, followed by Ivy and me walking side by side. Spencer was a few paces back. It was kind of hard not to stare at Ty since he was walking right in front of us. But basically, he ignored Ivy and me about as much as we ignored Spencer.

Oh well.

Once we made it past the junior high, I remembered Mom's suggestion. "Hey, we should do a sleepover sometime."

Ivy bit her lip. "It sounds fun, but, well . . . " Her voice didn't sound like she thought it would be fun at all.

But, well, what? I thought. Now I was wishing I hadn't even asked.

Ivy continued. "See, I can't have anyone over right now. Mom works a lot."

I let out a deep breath. *Was that all?* "I meant for you to come over to *my* house. Maybe Friday. Mom said she'd call your mom and work it all out. But if you don't want to . . . "

"Oh, I do," she said.

"Good." I tried to sound calm, but inside I was screaming, WOOOOHOOOO! Ivy wrote down her phone number, and I stuck it in my pocket.

As we walked on—and I stared—Ty reached into his pocket and pulled out a pack of gum.

"Can I have some?" Ivy asked.

Spencer stuck out his hand. "Me too?"

I was about to give Spencer "the look"—he's

very familiar with it, because he sees it every time I'm irritated with him. But before I could, Ty slowed his pace, took several pieces of gum from the pack, then handed one to Spencer, Ivy, and me.

As his hand dropped the small rectangular piece of gum into mine, the whoosh and roar of the passing school bus blew my hair into my face. My hand almost dropped the morsel of wrapped gum when I reached up to pull the hair from my face. That's when my eyes made eye contact with Celeste Holt, whose nose was pressed against the bus window.

Time seemed to slow, as if each tick of some silent clock kept rhythm with each breath I took. Tick—Ty's hand met mine. Tock—the bus whooshed by. Tick—I could almost hear Celeste's voice—*Who is that cute guy?* Tock—*And why is he walking home with Allie?*

● ● ● ● ●

Dear Allie,

How's my Cracker Jack girl? (Dad always called me this because he said I was full of surprises). So Mom mentioned in her e-mail yesterday that you'd had a little trouble in the cafeteria the other day. One of the other kids made a remark that upset you. Something about me coming home from Iraq and shooting someone?

Allie, one thing you're going to learn in this life—

and it sounds like you're getting a pretty good start there in the sixth grade—is that people (especially when they know nothing of what they are talking about) can say some really stupid things. The only thing I can figure is that in some way they must feel pretty bad about themselves to say something untrue and nasty about someone else.

It sounds like this Celeste girl doesn't really know you well, and she certainly doesn't know me. Don't let the ugly things that come out of her mouth give her power over you. Since she doesn't really know either of us, her words about us hold no value.

Now, you, on the other hand—you're the one who holds value in my life. Don't you forget it! I love you, Cracker Jack! Those are three words you can place a whole cafeteria full of value in. Give Mom, Spencer, and Tommy a big hug and kiss for me.

Love, Dad

6

One Ham-Hock of a Day

It was Thursday night—the day before Ivy was coming over—and it had been what Grandma would call "one ham-hock of a day." Celeste was pouty and whiny the entire day. Funny thing was, she never spoke directly to me, just pretended I wasn't there. She'd talk to the air, or stare out the window at the junior high and say stupid things like, "Wouldn't it be nice if the seventh grade boys practiced baseball during our recess? It's such a pain being surrounded by fifth and sixth grade boys—I feel like I'm at nursery school."

Whatever!

All I had to say was, fine with me! She could talk to herself all she wanted. It was bad enough having to face her perfect, popular face all day. The last thing I wanted to do was talk to it.

When I finally got home from school, Grandma was in the kitchen baking something that smelled incredible. She was good at that.

"Sweetie, time to feed Chewie," Grandma said.

Of all the names in the universe, we decided to call our baby goat Chewie, partly because Spencer's favorite dessert is chewy brownies, partly because my favorite desert is chewy chocolate chip cookies, but mostly because Dad's favorite movie is *Star Wars* and his favorite character is Chewbacca—Chewie—the furry, tall thing that doesn't talk but makes this funny vibrating noise. It just seemed to make sense. And it felt good to bring something about Dad into the decision.

I was tired from a long day at school—even hungry. But I figured I'd put "worst things first," as Grandma always said, and go feed our little goat. (I know—it's really "first things first," but Grandma looks at life a little different.)

After making up the bottle the way Grandma taught me, I went out back to find Chewie.

"What ya doing?" Spencer hollered from the tire swing.

I held up the bottle that looked like a baby bottle, only bigger. "What does it look like I'm doing?"

"Can I help?" Spencer asked.

"You can help me find Chewie," I hollered back. I couldn't see him anywhere. Or Abe, for that matter. Where had those two goats run off to? It's not like they could get far. The back field was fenced.

Spencer ran past me to the gate, opened it, and stuck his head through. He was a little leery about entering the field without me, though. He was still afraid that Abe might chase him. But not me. Abe and I had an understanding. I gave him Grandma's chocolate chip cookies once in a while, and he didn't chase me around the field. A perfect arrangement, if you ask me.

When I came to the gate, we both walked through and stared at the empty field. At the far side, the chickens were doing whatever it was that chickens do when they hang out in a chicken coop all day—laying eggs, and laying around, I suppose.

"I don't see 'em anywhere," said Spencer.

"This is *not* good," I said, more to myself, than anyone.

"Why?"

"Because if we can't see them, they must have gotten out somehow." Sheesh, my brother could be dense sometimes.

"Where'd they go?"

"How the heck would I know? Now will you stop asking dumb questions and go get Grandma? Hurry!"

Spencer ran back toward the house while I headed to the chicken coop. Maybe those crazy goats were in there with the chickens. Abe sure seems to love those little guys, always wanting to protect them, and I swear, I'll never understand why. When we first came here from Killeen, Abe wouldn't let me or Spencer anywhere near that chicken coop, at least not without a good chase. Crazy goat.

I opened the door to the coop and walked in—no goats. Where could they be? Just as I was about to leave, I thought I heard Chewie making his little baby goat sounds. I turned around toward the chickens, hoping that maybe my eyes hadn't seen things right, but they had. Just a bunch of hens sitting in their boxes, and that ornery rooster pacing the floor. No goats.

But then I heard it again. "Baaaaah." Baby goats sound an awful lot like sheep. But that was no sheep!

It was coming from behind the chicken coop. Funny, because I never realized there *was* a behind to the chicken coop.

After closing the door, I headed around the side and then to the back. Sure enough, there was a little walking space behind the coop, but the bushes next to the fence seemed to fill in most of the space. I wasn't too comfortable about walking back there until I saw the bushes rustling. Little Chewie's head peeked out, and once again he made his little goat noises.

"Chewie, get over here!" I hollered. But he wouldn't come.

Now I could hear another goat baaaahing. Abe!

I moved away the branches and leaves from the small path as I made my way behind the coop. I had no idea why two goats would be hiding behind the chicken coop. Maybe they were playing hide-and-go-seek. Well, all I had to say about that was, *gotcha!*

When I finally made it to Chewie, he went for the bottle in my hand and started sucking. Man, you'd think he was starved. I stroked his soft neck and gave him a kiss.

"You scared me—I thought you'd run away. Now where's Abe?"

"Baaaaaaah." As if answering my question, Abraham Lincoln, Grandma's watch goat, let out another sound, right behind the bush where I was kneeling.

I moved the leaves, and there was Abe, lying on his side next to the fence. When he saw me, he stood up, revealing an opening in the fence, just the right size for a baby goat like Chewie to escape.

"I don't believe it," I said to myself. I heard someone opening the door to the chicken coop.

"Allie, is that you back there?" It was Grandma.

"I found the goats," I said. "And you're never going to believe this."

"Well, come on out of there, and tell me all about it.

I picked up Chewie, still sucking at that bottle, and carried him out from behind the hen house. Grandma was there with Spencer, and Mom wasn't far behind with Tommy in her arms.

Spencer waved and began jumping. "You found Chewie," he said.

"Where's Abe?" Grandma asked.

At hearing her voice, Abe wandered out from behind the coop and went right to Grandma. "Now, what were you doing behind there, you silly?" Grandma asked

"He was trying to keep Chewie from running away," I said.

"How do you figure that?" Grandma asked.

"There's a hole in the fence back there big enough for Chewie to escape. I think he was trying to, but Abe blocked the hole—wouldn't budge."

Grandma scratched behind Abe's ears. "Well, my goodness, Abe. You're a hero."

"Just like Daddy," Spencer said.

I nodded.

● ● ● ● ●

Dear Dad,

It's been one ham-hock of a week! I'm so glad it's almost Friday because my friend Ivy (who I hope will be my best friend someday) gets to stay the night. I love having an almost-best friend!

Did I tell you about our new baby goat? We named him Chewie and he's really cute and sweet. He thinks I'm his mom and Abe is his dad. Abe thinks he's his dad too. Abe protects him like you protect me.

I love you, Dad!

Love, Allie, your Cracker Jack girl!

7

The Bright Side of Midnight

April was a weird month in places like Edna, Idaho. Some days you knew summer was just two short months away. And other days you were sure winter had switched to a year-round event. Today was one of those "other" days. It was cold enough that Grandma took pity on Spencer and me and picked us up after school. And since it was the day of the sleepover, Ivy was with us.

"Thanks, Grandma," I said. "We weren't looking forward to walking home in this weather." The three of us crawled into the back of Grandma's dark blue car. It was big and old. Mom always said a car like that could only belong to a grandma or a gangster.

"It's cold outside, that's for sure," Grandma said. "Might even snow tonight."

"Cool," Ivy's eyes widened. "I've hardly ever seen snow."

"Know what I heard today?" Spencer hollered while bouncing up and down next to me. The kid couldn't hold still for ten seconds.

"What?" Grandma asked.

"I heard that in some places like Alaska, or the North Pole, you can spit, and it'll turn to ice before it hits the ground."

"You don't say," Grandma said. Only Grandma—and Spencer—could think that frozen spit was an interesting topic of conversation.

"That's totally disgusting." I shot a glance at Spencer—still bouncing.

"No," Grandma corrected. "That's Mother Nature. And she's working overtime today. I'm a little worried about the animals tonight. It's just too cold. The chickens will be fine in the coop. I sealed it up good. And Abe does okay if I put him in the shed with some extra hay. But I don't think little Chewie can handle the cold weather we're going to get tonight, even if I put him with Abe."

This was definitely something to be worried about. We'd only had the baby goat for a few days, but I'd already become attached to him. You'd think with all the hard work involved in raising a baby goat, I'd be sick of it. Between me, Grandma, and Spencer, we had to bottle feed Chewie every four hours. Grandma took the middle of the night shift since we had school the next day. Mom didn't help because she already had her own baby to feed.

Spencer's bouncing became even more irritating. "Can Chewie sleep with me—*please?* There's lots of room in my bed."

"No, sir." Grandma was shaking her head. "Not in your bed. But if you'd like, I can fix the two of you a spot in the mud room. I'll leave the back door to the house open and keep the wood burning stove stoked. You and Chewie will stay warm for the night."

"How about me and Ivy?" I asked and looked over at Ivy. She smiled and nodded. I knew it—another thing in common. We were both animal lovers. "Can we sleep in the mud room with Chewie too?"

For some reason I almost expected Spencer to complain, but he didn't seem to mind.

"Cool," he said. "A slumber party."

There was no way any slumber party involving my little brother could be considered cool. But Ivy and I would make the best of it. We were learning to make do when things were sometimes miserable.

Just before the sun went down, we prepared Grandma's animals for the cold night ahead. The chickens were sealed up tight in the hen house, and Abe was snuggled in the shed, surrounded by lots of hay.

That left little Chewie. We'd spent all afternoon transforming the mud room into kid paradise (after all, a baby goat *is* called a kid). First we took a stack of newspapers and spread them all over the floor. Then we took a bunch of old blankets Grandma gave us and made a tent. We figured if human kids liked to sleep in tents, animal kids would love it too. Besides, it would help to keep us warm. Finally, we found some snacks that we'd all enjoy—crackers, carrots, and raisins. It wasn't a hot fudge sundae, but it would have to do.

We took shifts before bedtime watching Chewie. While Spencer had his turn, Ivy and I decided to go up to my room and hang out. Since we were spending the rest of the night with two little "kids," we decided to have some girl time. That's what Mom calls it when it's just me and her—no little brothers to ruin things.

"So this is my room—whoopdee-doo," I said as I spun around and threw my body onto my bed. I looked up at the cracked plaster ceiling. "How many sixth grade girls do you know who share a room with their first grade brother?"

I felt the bed shift as Ivy sat down next to me. "It's not so bad," she said.

"Yeah. It is."

Ivy looked around my room, and I wished I still had my light green comforter from back in Killeen. My bed here had one of Grandma's homemade quilts.

"At least you get your own bed," Ivy said. "Right now, I share with my mom. And Ty sleeps in the bed next to us."

I sat up next to Ivy and looked into her eyes. "Serious?"

She nodded, then looked down at her feet. "We're living at the Tidwell Motel right now—it's just temporary though," she added in a rush.

"What's it like?" I probably shouldn't have asked, but I was curious.

"It's basically one room with two beds, a kitchen area, and a bathroom. We're only there till school's out."

"Then what?"

"Then my mom marries Farmer Dirk. They met online—can you believe it?"

"Wow." My life was starting to feel normal.

"After the wedding, we're moving out to his place, and me and Ty each get our own room."

I raised my eyebrows. "His name is Farmer Dirk?"

"That's what me and Ty call him. He's a farmer and his first name is Dirk." Ivy shrugged her shoulders. "Farmer Dirk." Then her voice became soft. "Besides, there's no way I'm going to call him Dad—already got one of those."

"Where does your dad live?"

"Back home in Elk Grove. But he married Stephanie a little over a year ago. They just had a new baby girl, Emma. She's real cute." Ivy's voice was low and dull. It didn't sound happy like mine did when I talk about my baby brother, Tommy.

"Whoa." I didn't know what more to say. I guess Ivy didn't either because she threw herself back on my bed. Now she was looking at the cracks, so I joined her.

We were both quiet for a moment, staring at my hundred-year-old ceiling. Ivy's voice broke the silence. "I lived in the same house, and had the same bedroom, from the day I was born until I turned ten. That's when my life went crazy."

"What happened?"

"My mom and dad got a divorce. Didn't even bother to ask me or Ty how we felt about it. Just Splitsville."

"I'm sorry."

"Me too." Ivy let out a deep sigh.

Neither of us spoke again for a bit—just stared at those cracks. I could tell Ivy was feeling sad. I wanted to say something to make her feel a little better, but I wasn't sure what. I didn't have divorced parents. But I *did* know what it was like to be far away from a parent. My dad had been gone so long, it felt like forever—plus two more months! Maybe Ivy felt the same being so far from her dad.

The cracks were starting to get boring, so I rolled over on my side, put my elbow up on the bed, and propped my head in my hand. "I don't get to see my dad until July—how about you?"

"August. By then the baby will be older. Stephanie and Dad think it'll be a better time for me and Ty to be there." Ivy rolled onto her side. We were now facing each other, and for the first time I noticed her wet eyes. "My dad's life is so busy with Stephanie and now baby Emma. There doesn't seem room for me. Or Ty—well, except for two stinkin' weeks in August." Ivy wiped her eyes and then blinked.

I wanted to think of something to make Ivy feel better. This was a sleepover. We were supposed to be having fun! On the other hand, I knew better than anyone what it was like coming to a new place—being the new kid, missing my dad.

"I'm sure your dad misses you a ton. I know in his e-mails, *my* dad says that he thinks about me every day. I bet it's the same with yours."

Ivy didn't say anything, just shrugged.

"So let's look on the bright side," I said, sounding way too much like Grandma. It was a little scary, but after a year of living with her, she was rubbing off on me. Maybe that wasn't such a bad thing. Grandma was pretty cool, as far as grandmas go. She always says she can find the "bright side of midnight."

"And what would 'the bright side' be?" Ivy asked.

I hopped up onto my knees. A plan was hatching in my brain about as fast as I could think and speak. It was brilliant! "The bright side is that the two of us only have three months together before I leave—well, that's not the bright side— but we're going to make this the very best summer in the history of very best friends having very best summers that Edna, Idaho, has ever seen." I knew it sounded strange. I even threw in the 'very best friend' part. What the heck. I only had three months so I had to act fast.

There was a lot of meaning in my words—if they were understood by the right person, that is. Someone who felt alone. Someone who missed their dad. Ivy and me—we were more alike now than I'd ever imagined.

Grandma always said that God brings people together at certain times and in certain places because they need each other. Earth's angels, she calls them. Well, Ivy and I—we were each other's Earth angels. God must have known that we needed each other this summer.

A slow smile spread across Ivy's face. She understood. With one last blink of her eyes, the sadness disappeared. Now Ivy was up on her knees too.

"We need to make a plan," she said.

"A 'best summer for best friends' plan," I said.

"Yeah . . . " Ivy nodded her head. Excitement filled her voice. "And even though it's only April, let's start right here. Right now."

"With this sleepover," I said. "And we'll have more all summer long."

"Hey, I thought of another bright side," said Ivy.

"What?"

"I'll even have my own bedroom for our sleepovers after Mom marries Farmer Dirk. Oh, and he has a trampoline—maybe we can sleep out on the trampoline this summer!"

I laughed. "Oh, that sounds fun. What's his house like?"

"I've only been there once, but it was dark out so I couldn't see much. Basically it's just a plain old white house out in the country—looks like a rectangle. We're eating dinner there tomorrow night so I'll check it out. Mom says Dirk's a good cook—I guess from living alone all these years." Ivy's eyes suddenly grew wide. "Hey, you want to come with us?"

"To Farmer Dirk's?"

"For Sunday dinner. Please? It'll be fun."

"Sure, if it's okay."

"It will be."

● ● ● ● ●

Mental e-mail to Dad—the one I'm afraid to send:

Dear Dad,

I'm glad you're my dad. Please come home safe from Iraq. I know some soldiers have died over there. I don't want you to die too. I only want one dad—you!

Love, Allie

8

When Life Throws a Punch, Remember to Duck

My sleepover with Ivy and Chewie was a blast, even with Spencer around. The kid (my brother, that is) fell asleep fast, thank goodness. And after Ivy and I fed Chewie a bottle, the critter fell asleep between us on a pile of blankets. We both agreed he was such a sweet and cute little goat, and I almost felt like his mother, or maybe a big sister. Well, whatever I was to that goat, it felt good to be needed, and to love and care for someone else— even a baby goat.

Saturday started out very cold. Grandma let us bring Chewie in from the mud room, so we all huddled in front of the wood-burning stove in the living room and watched cartoons. Good times! The sun came out and the day slowly warmed. I knew it would be a great day.

At six o'clock that evening, feeling both exhausted and excited, Ivy and I slid into the back seat of Mrs. Peterson's car and headed to Farmer Dirks house for dinner. As soon as we got into the car, I realized Ty was in the front seat.

"Did you two have a nice sleepover?" Ivy's mom asked.

"Yes, ma'am," I said.

Ivy gave me a funny look. "Ma'am?" She laughed for some reason. I just shrugged.

"Ivy tells me you're from Texas," Mrs. Peterson said.

"We lived in Killeen before we came here. It's kind of near the middle of the state."

Ty turned around in his seat. "You don't sound like you're from Texas—well, except for the ma'am part."

He was talking to me. Ty Peterson—Mr. Hottie—was talking to *me!* I hadn't told Ivy I thought her brother was the next best thing to nachos smothered in melted cheese. I didn't want her to think *he* was the reason we were friends. I thought of him as a bonus prize.

"How are people in Texas supposed to sound?" Ivy asked. I was grateful because at the moment, my tongue felt like a brick.

"They sound like this." Ty made his mouth slant to the side. "Howdy, y'all. I'm fixin' to have supper with Farmer Dirk tonight. Y'all wanna come along and eat some vittles?"

"We don't talk like that," I said, a smile tugging at the corner of my mouth. I looked at Ty with those blue eyes. Who could be mad at blue eyes?

Ivy scrunched up her nose. "I am *so* not eating vittles, whatever that is! It sounds slimy . . . and nasty."

We all laughed.

"You have nothing to worry about," Mrs. Peterson said as she turned her head slightly to talk to her daughter while still keeping an eye on the road. " 'Vittles' is just an old-fashioned term for food—and I don't think anyone in Texas has used it for a hundred years." I noticed the quick glance Mrs. Peterson shot to her son. "And you," she said. "You're a goofball. Will you *please* stop calling my fiancé Farmer Dirk? I know you're joking around, but it comes across disrespectful."

"Then what are we supposed to call him?" Ty asked. "Daddy Dirk?"

Ivy sat up straight. "I've told you—I'm *not* calling him 'dad.'"

"Calm down. No one has asked you to. Just call him whatever makes you feel comfortable. That's what Dirk wants—for you to be comfortable around him. He's never been married before—never had kids. He really is trying his best. I'd like you two to do the same."

Ivy looked at me and rolled her eyes. I gave a weak smile. I wasn't sure what else to do at the moment. I couldn't imagine being in her situation. Sure, my dad had been away for almost a year, and I missed him so much it made me cry some nights. But at least he was my 'one and only' dad. I couldn't imagine how confusing it would be to have *two* dads. It was hard enough having two brothers. And two goats.

We drove quite a ways out on a dark country road until we came to Farmer Dirk's house. I made a mental note *not* to call Ivy's future stepdad Farmer Dirk. But since I didn't know his last name, I decided to return to my Texas ways and just call him "sir." If I got teased by Ty and Ivy later, then as Grandma would say, "When life throws a punch, remember to duck."

Ivy had been right. Farmer Dirk's house looked like a white rectangle, but it had a garage sticking out at the end. It was a nice house, though—not brand new, but not ancient either. Definitely not as old as Grandma's big yellow house, that's for sure! I had a feeling Ivy would like living there. I had no idea what her house in California was like, but this had to be better than sharing a room with her mom and brother at the Tidwell Motel.

Once the car came to a stop, Ivy's mom turned around to face us.

"I forgot to mention that Dirk's sister and her family will be joining us for dinner. They live next door. Over there."

Mrs. Peterson pointed to the house "next door," which was more like a half a football field down the road. Now *that* was a nice house! Big for Edna, Idaho, standards, and much newer. It was lit up by several outdoor lights. It was beautiful.

Ty pointed to the lit-up house. "Are they farmers too?"

"No. Dirk's brother-in-law owns a quarry in the hills east of town. See the rock on the outside of the house? It's called Edna rock. It's sold all over the country."

Ty turned to his mom. "Remind me to own a quarry when I grow up."

Mrs. Peterson groaned as she pulled the baseball cap off of her son, whacked his head with it, then placed it back onto his head. And she did it with a smile on her face.

"Come on, kids. Let's go eat some vittles!"

The four of us got out of the car and walked toward the house. I was anxious to see the inside of Ivy's new house—scope things out for what was going to be an incredible summer of incredible sleepovers. I could feel it!

Before Mrs. Peterson had a chance to knock on the door, a large man wearing a baseball cap, jeans, a plaid shirt, and cowboy boots opened the door. A huge smile lit his face when his eyes landed on Ivy's mom. Her face looked pretty much the same. As Grandma would say, *they're sharing a honey sandwich and it's sticking to everything!*

I think it embarrassed Ivy that her mom and Farmer Dirk stayed in a hug a little longer than I'd ever feel comfortable hugging a guy (well, besides my dad).

Ivy let out a groan. "Mo-om!" She bellowed the word and it came out in two syllables.

The two adults quickly released their hug, but their smiles were still there. Who needed a porch light the way those two were shining? I'm not sure, but I don't think I'll ever understand love. At twelve, I was still getting used to the idea that someday a boy might kiss me. And if that boy was Ty Peterson, well, I don't think I'd mind . . . in a few years. Right now, the thought creeped me out a little.

After a quick introduction to Farmer Dirk, he waved his hand inside. "Come on in, everyone. I've got a few people I want you to meet."

As Farmer Dirk led the way into Ivy's future house, Ivy and I hung back a bit and she whispered into my ear. "I bet he's going to introduce us to our future new cousins from that big rock house. Oh boy, just what I need—pretend cousins."

"I think they'd be your stepcousins," I corrected.

"Whatever. I *told* you my life was crazy!"

"Well, whatever you want to call them, there's one thing you're forgetting."

"What?"

"If they live in that nice big rock house, maybe they have other nice, big things—like a PS3, a widescreen TV, a swimming pool and Jacuzzi."

Ivy's expression began to change.

"Remember what I said last night. There's always a bright side!"

Ivy rolled her eyes. "You sound like your grandma."

"I know," I said with a laugh. "Scary, isn't it?"

Ivy laughed.

The two of us fell behind the others, lost in our world of best-friend gossip. We were still wandering through the living room but could now hear introductions being made down the hall and around the corner in what I assumed was a family room.

Ivy's mom and Ty were saying hi, as well as another man and woman—obviously adults. But then I heard another voice. A familiar voice. It wasn't Ty . . . or Mrs. Peterson. But I knew that voice well, if not better than even Ivy's voice.

When we rounded the corner into the family room, everyone turned toward us. I suddenly felt self-conscious, like I had chocolate on my lips. Or worse yet, a booger stuck to my face. I wiped my nose, just in case.

"There they are," said Mrs. Peterson. "This is my daughter Ivy and her friend Allie. Girls, this is Dirk's sister, Connie, her husband Mark, and their daughter, Celeste. Maybe you two know her from school. You're probably close to the same age."

Neither of us said anything—just stared. Stared at Celeste. Celeste Holt. Our worst enemy at Edna Elementary School. Our worst enemy in the universe. And Ivy's soon-to-be stepcousin.

I didn't even need to ask—I just knew.

We both wanted to puke.

● ● ● ● ●

Dear Allie,

I'm sorry it's been one ham-hock of a week. (You're starting to sound like Grandma.) I've had a few of those weeks myself lately. But when things start to get

me down I think of home—you, Spencer, Tommy, and
Mom. Anywhere the four of you are, that's where I want
to be too. July will come soon. Just stay busy taking care
of Chewie and playing with your friends. Time will
pass quickly.

I love you, Cracker Jack!

Love, Dad

9

Nightmare at Farmer Dirk's

Dinner at Farmer Dirk's turned out to be the *nightmare* at Farmer Dirk's. Seriously, how much worse could it get than to discover your soon-to-be stepcousin and next-door neighbor was the girl who, for some reason, took personal responsibility to make your new life at your new school totally miserable?

All I had to say was, *poor Ivy!*

Celeste stayed true to herself and basically ignored Ivy and me the entire dinner, focusing all attention on Ty—big surprise there. The adults never even noticed. Farmer Dirk arranged for the adults to eat in the dining room and the kids in the kitchen. Lucky us!

Ivy and I slurped our spaghetti while Celeste tried to slurp up as much attention as she could get from Ty. And the whole time she didn't even eat. Just held this black cat with freaky gold eyes in one arm and stroked it with the other. Only one thought came to my mind—she *must* be a witch.

"So, Ty, what position in baseball do you play?" "So, Ty, what's California like?" And our favorite, "So, Ty, have you ever been surfing?" Puh-leeze!

Poor Ty. He kept shoveling spaghetti in his mouth like he was half-starved. I think so he wouldn't have to talk. And the witch—she just ignored us and focused on Ty and the cat. From where we were sitting two feet away, it didn't look like her magic was working. But then, you never know with guys.

I suppose that's why I was so surprised on Monday morning when I sat down at my desk. It was five minutes before class started, and Mrs. Kaneko was busy at the other side of the room sorting through a file cabinet. Celeste was also early, and that's when the craziest of crazy things happened. Celeste started talking to me . . . like we were almost friends or something.

"It's kind of funny," she said, "that Ivy and Ty's mom is marrying my uncle Dirk—don't you think?"

"Yeah," I half mumbled, mostly because I was in shock that Celeste was actually speaking to me. And it wasn't even an insult. If I hadn't been so shocked, I might have totally freaked. It wasn't natural.

"That means they're going to be my cousins. How weird is that?"

"Stepcousins, and *way* weird," I replied.

"The only other cousins I have are on my dad's side and live in Kansas—I never see them."

"Never?"

"Almost never."

I hardly knew how to reply. "Hmmm..."

Celeste leaned forward, resting her arms on the desk. "So did Ty say anything about me after the dinner?"

So *that's* what this was about. "Uh . . . no."

Celeste took a deep breath before turning her gaze to the window and the empty junior high baseball field across the street. I could only guess who she was looking for and his name started with a *T* and ended with a *Y*. Go figure.

Celeste flipped her hair with her hands and turned her attention back to our classroom and planet earth. Bummer. I kind of liked it when she was in her own universe.

"It'll be nice having cousins living nearby. I don't have any brothers or sisters. It's just me, Mom and Dad, and Uncle Dirk. Oh, and Harry."

"Harry?"

"Harry Potter."

"You like to read?" Why did this surprise me?

"No, my cat."

"Your cat likes to read?"

Celeste let out a deep, noisy breath. "Harry is the black cat at Uncle Dirk's."

"Oh. Yeah. I remember." I didn't mention that the cat's gold eyes totally creeped me out.

"Uncle Dirk bought him for me last year, but he knows how much my mom freaks about animals, so he lets me keep him at his house."

"That's nice," I said. *And a little weird.*

"He's my best friend," she said.

How do you respond to that? I didn't, just made a mental note: *maybe my life isn't so bad.*

Mrs. Kaneko started class. After the pledge, roll, and announcements from Principal Barnes, we were told to quietly walk to the library. Celeste hurried over to Tiffany and Aubrey, and the trio hugged like lost children at the mall, finally reunited with their mommy. Ugh!

When I met up with Ivy at the coat rack, she raised one eyebrow. "Celeste is talking to you?"

"Only about your brother and that freaky black cat."

"The one at Farmer Dirk's?"

"Yeah, she said her mom hates cats or something, so it has to live there, even though it's hers."

"Until *I* move in and win it over," Ivy said with a grin. "Animals love me."

The look in Ivy's eyes made me laugh.

At the library, we wandered the aisles looking for a book to check out. I found one right away—I always choose a book by the cover. But Ivy read the back of every book she picked up. I was tired of waiting.

"I'm going to check out," I said.

She nodded but continued reading.

Just before I reached the checkout desk, my eyes were drawn to a magazine rack. Something familiar reached out from one of the covers, grabbed me right around the heart, and squeezed so tight I could hardly breathe.

The room began to spin. I sat down right on the floor in front of the rack and stared at the guy on the cover. He looked so much like Dad, dressed in his cammies. Dad wore his army clothes almost every day. When I touched the cover, I felt the stiff material of Dad's shirt. His smell came right off of the cover—the one right after he showered. The best time to give Dad a hug.

But my dad's look-alike had a big gun clenched in his fists and a helmet on his head. He wore Dad's "serious thinking" look on his face. He wasn't saying "cheese," that's for sure. I don't think he even knew a camera was there.

The cover read, "*Fighting a War*, story on page 39." Part of me wanted to open that magazine and read page 39. But another part wanted to ignore it. I was afraid of what it might say, how it might make me feel. The pages shook in my hands.

I jumped when something touched my shoulder. "I'm sorry. I didn't mean to startle you." When I looked up, Mrs. Pack, the school librarian, was standing next to me. "Is everything okay?"

"Sure," I lied. "Can I check out this magazine?" I asked. If I was going to read page 39, I sure didn't want to do it surrounded by every kid in the sixth grade.

"I'm sorry. The magazines can't be checked out. But you're welcome to come in and read them right here in the library."

A lot of help that was. "Oh, okay."

I slowly stood and placed my dad's look-alike back on the shelf. I knew I'd be back. When I was ready.

I couldn't stay away now.

● ● ● ● ●

Dear Dad,

I thought I saw you today on the cover of a magazine, but it was someone who looked like you. Another soldier. The cover said Fighting a War. I don't like to think about these words because it makes me worry about you. I hope you're safe.

Everything is going great in Edna. Ivy is my best friend and for the first time I think I like living in Edna. How weird is that? But I'm still looking forward to seeing you again.

Please be safe!

Love, Allie

10

Truth and Truce

A year ago, when I first found out Mom was pregnant, for some reason I started noticing babies. Everywhere. Even before they were born. Women with huge baby-filled bellies waddled around every corner. At the grocery store, babies sucked on the handle of every cart—gross. At church their cries screeched in my ears. Even diaper commercials had me staring at the TV.

That's how it was now with Dad and Iraq. He'd been there for nearly a year and mostly I just missed him. But now it felt more real. My dad's look-alike on the cover of that magazine changed me. I needed to know more.

It started small. Willy Simms wore a cammie t-shirt to school. "Support Our Troops" ribbon-shaped stickers were stuck on cars. And American flags flew all over Edna. These things were okay—even good.

But then there were bigger things. Things that made my insides dizzy. Like the newspaper box in front of Brown's grocery store. Every day when I walked past, newspaper headlines about Iraq screamed out at me. Sometimes I didn't understand the words—insurgents, Sunnis, IEDs. But I always understood the pictures. That voice was clear. *War is ugly.*

One morning as I entered the kitchen, a reporter on the morning news, dressed in a helmet and bulky black vest, was talking to a soldier. Something about a car bomb.

I stood still outside the kitchen door. I wanted to hear more. But Mom turned around from the table, grabbed the remote, and flipped the TV off.

"Morning, sweetie." Her voice was *way* too cheerful.

"Why do you do that?" I snapped.

"What?"

"You always turn the news off when I come in the room."

"We don't need to watch TV while we're eating breakfast."

I dropped into the chair across from Mom. "You do it all the time. Whenever they're talking about Iraq you turn off the TV. How am I supposed to find out what's happening over there? How am I supposed to find out if Dad is okay?"

I didn't mean to start crying. I was more mad than sad. But when I said Dad's name, my voice gave in to that empty place inside of me. That place where Dad belonged.

Mom stood up and I wondered for a moment if I'd made her mad. But her arms wrapped around me from behind like a big warm blanket and snuggled me in. Her head rested on my shoulder.

While my body shook, letting out sobs and tears, Mom was there to hold me, quiet me.

"Shhhhh. Daddy's okay," she said as we rocked from side to side.

"But how do I *know*?" I cried. "No one ever tells me—especially you."

"I don't think any of us really know. Not even the guys on the news." Mom whispered the words into my ear.

"Then who does?" I asked.

"The soldiers," Mom said. "Daddy."

Mom's words felt comforting. I still wanted to read page 39 of that library magazine. And I still wanted to watch the news. But I've always trusted my dad. He knew what he was doing when he decided to be a soldier. Dad said it's who he is. What he stands for.

I didn't want my dad to be *anyone* else. So I suppose right now, he couldn't be *anywhere* else.

By the time I arrived at school, it had already been a long day. Who wants to start their day with a big bawl? I hoped my eyes weren't puffy. If they were, Celeste would let me know.

Ugh—Celeste. The thought of staring at Her Royal Witchness for the next seven hours didn't have me doing cartwheels. We talked to each other now, but only during class. Never at recess. Definitely not at lunch. She had Tiffany and Aubrey. I had Ivy. That was enough.

"Want to hear something funny?" Celeste said as soon as I sat down.

Did I have a choice? "Funny's good," I replied.

"A few weeks ago when I saw you walking home with Ivy and Ty, I thought that maybe Ty was your boyfriend or something. How funny is that?"

"Way funny," I said, only I didn't sound amused. I mean, what would be so funny about me having a boyfriend? Not that I wanted one or anything, but it was hardly something to laugh your guts out about, right? I didn't need this.

Celeste continued. "I'd seen Ty with the seventh grade boys, but I didn't know he was Ivy's brother till the three of you came to Uncle Dirk's house for dinner. That's when I put two and two together."

"I guess you get an A plus in math, then—good for you, Einstein."

Celeste straightened her back and looked into my eyes for probably the first time this entire conversation. "You want math, Allie Claybrook? Well, here you go. Number one—your eyes are puffy. Not a good look on you. And number two— I'm not stupid. I know you and Ivy don't like me. And I'm not a member of your fan club either, especially after what happened in the cafeteria with that green stuff." As Celeste spoke of that moment, her nose scrunched up.

I couldn't hide my smile at the mention of the cafeteria and the green bean handshake. Sure, it landed me in "jail" with Celeste the rest of the school year, but it *was* funny. Celeste didn't think so. I could have sworn her eyes were starting to tear up. But she blinked a few times and turned back toward the window and the empty baseball diamond across the road.

Did the princess-witch actually have feelings?

Now *I* felt bad. Why did I have to have a conscience? In her own unique and slightly twisted way, Celeste tried to reach out to me. She was the one who started our weird "talking-in-the-classroom-only" semi-friendship. And now I'd shoved it back into her face. Maybe I didn't have to be best friends with the girl (besides, that position had been filled when Ivy came to town), but I could at least try to understand her. After all, she was going to be Ivy's stepcousin. That made us almost related.

Before I'd chicken out, I held my right hand across our desks, in true handshake fashion. Celeste didn't notice so I cleared my throat.

She turned her eyes toward my face, then to my hand. I wasn't quite sure if she looked irritated or confused.

"I'd like to call a truce," I said.

Celeste leaned back in her chair and folded her arms. "And that means . . . ?"

"It means I think that you and me and Ivy shouldn't be enemies anymore. It just doesn't make sense—especially since you and Ivy are going to be stepcousins in a few more weeks."

I was about to say more, but the school bell rang and Mrs. Kaneko started talking about permission slips for an upcoming field trip. I sat down and tried to pay attention . . . but it was useless. What had I done?

I couldn't bear to look over at Celeste. The girl probably thought I was the biggest dweeb in the universe. I'm sure she was probably laughing her popular pants off. And if I thought things were bad now, I could only imagine how it would be at recess. She'd be surrounded by Tiffany and Aubrey on the playground, and they'd have a great time making fun of me. Celeste would stick out her hand and say, "Truce?" And even though it wasn't funny, Tiffany and Aubrey would laugh. They always laughed when Celeste was trying to be funny.

Now I was starting to fume. Not only was I embarrassed by what I was sure would happen at recess, but I was mad! Well, I'd show her . . .

In the middle of my argument with myself, something hit me on my chest, then fell into my lap. I looked down and it was a piece of paper folded into a small triangle. In tiny print it said: *You're psycho if you think I'll shake your hand.* Then it said, *OVER.*

I flipped the triangle over and nearly fell off my chair in the middle of Mrs. Kaneko's field trip speech.

Only one word was written—*truce.*

I looked across the desk at Celeste and she shrugged her shoulders, followed by something that surprised me more than anything.

She smiled.

● ● ● ● ●

Another mental e-mail to Dad that I'll probably never send:

Dear Dad,

Do you think a boy will ever like me the way you like mom? Does that seem like such a funny idea?

Love, Allie

P.S. I hope someone will call a truce in Iraq so you won't have to go back.

P.P.S. Do you have to like your enemy even if you've called a truce? I hope not.

11

The Clock Ticks Twice as Fast When You're Wearin' a Smile

Grandma always says, "The clock ticks twice as fast when you're wearin' a smile." Strange how Grandma is always right. The last few weeks of school went by so fast I hardly noticed. Maybe the truce with Celeste had something to do with it. Don't get me wrong, she wasn't my best friend. But she wasn't my enemy now.

She'd still say irritating things now and then, but I tried to ignore them. So did Ivy. Her mom was about to marry Celeste's uncle. Ivy was trying to keep peace in her family (or step-family) and I was trying to help.

Two days after school let out—the big day of the wedding—I dressed up in my best yellow dress and Mom drove me out to Celeste's house. No, I wasn't going to hang out with Celeste. Things hadn't changed *that* much. The wedding was being held in Celeste's backyard.

I had to admit, it was the perfect place for an outdoor wedding. Shade trees surrounded the yard with a big one plopped right in the middle like a huge green umbrella. It must have been there way longer than the house.

Several rosebushes and flowerbeds made the yard look like a colorful painting. I wasn't sure I'd ever seen a yard quite so beautiful, except maybe in pictures, or on the calendars Mom buys. When she dropped me off, she said the house was like her dream house. I agreed. It was beautiful.

"You look like one of those flowers," I said to Ivy as we stood next a rosebush. She was wearing a light purple dress with the bottom ruffled out like petals.

Ivy looked down and held out the skirt. "My mom's idea, not mine. I'm her maid of honor—whoopee."

"Well, I think it's pretty. You look great."

"Thanks," Ivy said, still looking down. Her voice sounded flat, sad.

It was still another half-hour before the wedding would start and I knew I needed to do something to help my best friend's mood, so I grabbed Ivy's arm. "Let's go for a walk."

The two of us wandered around Celeste's backyard. We were silent for a while . . . until I couldn't stand it any longer.

"What's wrong?"

Ivy studied the grass. "Today makes it real."

"Makes what real?"

She plucked a stray dandelion near a bush and examined it before blowing the fluff away. Then she dropped the stem and finally looked into my eyes. "My life—it'll never be the same as it used to be."

"Like back in California, when your mom and dad were married?"

"I don't understand why everything had to change. They say they weren't happy together—but *I* was. Doesn't that count for anything? Why didn't anyone ask what *I* thought—how *I* felt?" Tears began to well up in Ivy's eyes.

A fancy cement bench was parked under one of the shade trees at the edge of the yard. A few guests started to arrive on the other side of the yard and were seated under a huge white canopy. A man and two women played violins and a cello. There was no rush yet, so I directed Ivy to the bench. I sat next to her and locked my arm into hers. Grandma does this with me when we sit on the covered bench swing overlooking her vegetable garden. It always makes me feel happy—loved.

"My parents aren't divorced," I said. "But in a way I know how you feel." I didn't say anything for a minute, but neither did she, so I continued on. "I was perfectly happy back in Killeen. I liked my school. I liked Texas. And most of all, my dad was there with us. Then everything turned upside down—Dad left for Iraq and we moved here to Edna to live with Grandma. No one ever asked me my opinion on any of that either."

Ivy wiped at her eyes and sniffled. "Kinda sucks, doesn't it?"

At first I thought I knew how I wanted to respond, but my heart somehow started speaking to my brain and wouldn't let my mouth agree to what Ivy had just said. Bodies can be funny like that. Grandma would say they're automatic, like a burp—you just can't stop it. And if you do, you end up with a bellyache. I suppose that really is true.

"You know what?" I said. "At times it *has* sucked. Especially at first." Ivy was nodding, but I continued. "Mostly being away from my dad. But a lot of good things have come from being here in Edna."

Ivy looked over at me. "Like what?"

"Like my grandma—I never really knew her very well before. Never knew how cool and crazy she really was until I lived with her for a few months and got to know her better. She's way better than I ever imagined a grandma could be. Did you know she talks to her goat, Abe, and somehow he talks back? Seriously, they get all 'Dr. Dolittle' and communicate. I have no idea how. She'll probably start talking to Chewie next."

This brought a smile to Ivy's face. She'd been to the big yellow house and knew the goats. She'd seen Grandma with them and knew what I was talking about.

"And then there's my mom. Now I know it might sound crazy, but we're better friends now than we were a year ago back in Killeen."

Ivy didn't say anything, just nodded. She understood. She had the same kind of friendship with her mom. I'd seen it.

"And then there's you," I said. "We'd never have met if neither of us came to Edna. Of all the places in the universe, it's crazy how I meet my best friend here."

"Yeah, and you're leaving in July."

"You'll have Celeste and her freaky cat," I teased.

"That's *not* funny!" she said, and looked even more miserable.

"I'm sorry." And I really was. It totally stunk that I had to leave in July when I finally had a friend. "Hey, I know. I'll hide in your closet when it's time to leave. They'll never miss me." I was joking—sort of.

Finally, Ivy laughed. But it was one of those laughter-through-tears kind of laughs. "Sounds like a plan," she said, then sniffed.

We didn't say anything for a bit, just stared at the people all dressed up for the wedding.

"Mom sure seems happy to be marrying Dirk."

"A happy mom is *always* a good thing—another one of Grandma's sayings." Then I put some excitement in my voice. "And to top it off, you get Celeste Holt for a stepcousin—how cool is that?"

Ivy practically knocked me over with a nudge to my shoulder. "Gee, thanks for reminding me."

A grin spread across my face. "Hey, I know, maybe some day she'll marry Ty and actually become your sister-in-law."

Ivy nudged me again. This time I *did* lose my balance, but I braced my arm on the bench to stop the fall.

"It could happen," I said.

Ivy raised an eyebrow. All traces of tears disappeared. "Or he could marry you," she said. "Then *you'd* be my sister-in-law. I like that better."

The thought of this made my insides feel like a Fourth of July fireworks explosion. "No way!" I shrieked.

Ivy grinned. "It could happen."

"What could happen?"

Ty's voice came from behind us and might as well have been a tidal wave the way it nearly knocked us off the bench. We quickly recovered to our feet, clutching onto each other, as he walked up.

"You two okay?"

"Perfect," I said and shot Ivy a stern look. The last thing I needed was for her to spill the beans— my beans—about how I thought her brother was completely, and in every way, *hot!*

"Great, 'cause Mom needs you in the house— *now.*"

"C'mon." She leaned in and whispered, "Sis."

My finger shot up to my mouth. "Shhhhhh."

Ivy grabbed my arm in hers and we started toward the house. After a few steps I elbowed her in the ribs, playfully, of course.

"Ow!" she said, and bumped me with her hip.

"Hey . . . " I nudged her with my shoulder and we both laughed.

It was awesome having a best friend! I never wanted it to end.

The minute we entered Celeste's house, Ivy was rushed off by her grandma to get ready for her maid-of-honor duties, whatever those were. Ivy said all she had to do was stand next to her mom and not do anything stupid like faint or throw up. How difficult could it be?

I was about to walk back out to the yard and stare at more flowers, I suppose. But Celeste stopped me before I made it out the door.

"What are you doing in here?' she asked.

"Leaving." I was *not* in the mood to get into anything with Celeste. Especially today.

Celeste looked around, then lowered her voice. "Wanna see my bedroom?"

I had to admit, I was curious. This house was probably the most beautiful house I'd ever been in. Everything looked new. Matched perfectly. And it was clean. Even cleaner than Grandma's house, which is always clean except for little messes that Spencer makes. I suppose I make a few myself, but Grandma and Mom are always on us to pick up after ourselves.

The thing that was different about Celeste's house—aside from everything looking new—was that it didn't look lived in. It was just *too* perfect.

Still I couldn't help feeling jealous that Celeste Holt was the only kid to ever live in this house. It didn't seem fair, especially when I had to share a one-hundred-year-old attic room with a cracked and peeling ceiling with my first-grader brother. And worse yet, for the past month, Ivy shared a room at the Tidwell Motel with her mom and Ty.

Celeste waved her arm. "Hurry."

We walked up a giant white carpeted staircase that twisted around in a full circle by the time we were at the top. How cool was that? And how did they keep the carpet looking so white? Once Grandma told me that the green carpet on the stairs to my bedroom was almost as old as she was. I'm not sure, but I'd say that was almost considered an antique.

At the top of the circle staircase, Celeste opened a large wooden door, and I swear we walked into the bedroom of a princess, or, well . . . a dang lucky, spoiled rotten kid. Man, I wished it was me. But to be honest, it pretty much described Celeste Holt— both the dang lucky and the spoiled part (some would keep *rotten* in there, too).

If I thought the yard and the house were beautiful, the only way to describe Celeste's room was heavenly! The walls were a pale purple and rose higher than any bedroom ceiling I'd seen. And speaking of ceilings, this one wasn't just flat.

It rose from the walls in angles and met at the top of the ceiling to form a square.

The far wall was especially beautiful with a large oval stained glass window. What kind of kid has a room like this? Oh wait, we already discussed that.

"Whoa," I said and instinctively kicked off my sandals. I knew if I didn't walk barefoot across the lush lavender carpet, I'd regret it the rest of my life. My toes sunk into the surface, and as I walked toward the window I looked back to see if I'd left footprints, like on the sand. Crazy enough, I hadn't.

Celeste walked over to a white four-poster canopy bed and plopped herself on it. "Like my bedroom?" she asked.

"I've never, ever seen a room like this in my entire life," I nearly squealed. "Even in Texas," I added because some people think everything's bigger in Texas. I suppose it didn't count when it came to bedrooms. "You must *love* living here."

Celeste rolled over onto her back. "It's okay."

"It's *way* okay." My eyes were trying to calculate the number of porcelain dolls lined across the top of a bookshelf. I had *one* and it belonged to my mom when she was little.

A huge Barbie castle sat in the corner, and even though I was twelve years old, I had the sudden urge to skip the wedding and play Barbies for the

rest of the afternoon. So what if I was about to
enter junior high school in the fall? How often did
a girl get to play with a huge Barbie castle the size
of your average Volkswagen Bug? I bet if Grandma
and Mom were there, they'd forget about chores
and babies and want to play too.

"Has Ivy checked this out yet?" I asked,
fingering the detail on the outside of the castle.

"Nope."

"How about Tiffany and Aubrey? I bet they love
to hang out at your place." I suddenly understood
those two and their choice of friends better. There
were definitely perks to having Celeste as a friend.
Who wouldn't want to hang out with someone
who practically lived in a palace, at least by Edna
standards?

"They were here once. My birthday last
February."

"Once? You mean they've only been to your
house once?"

Celeste nodded; then her eyes grew wide.
"It was a slumber party. My first." Now she was
smiling. "We had so much fun. And we made a *huge*
mess of things." As quickly as her smile appeared,
it faded. "But Mom can't really deal with messes.
They haven't been back since. I usually just go over
to their places. It's easier that way. Besides, Aubrey
has horses."

Wow, I didn't know how to respond. It didn't seem right for a totally awesome bedroom to only be enjoyed by one kid. Half the fun of playing is having someone to play with. It made me wonder if Ivy would be allowed to hang out here after the wedding. They'd be stepcousins and next-door-neighbors after today. And even if she was allowed over, were messes totally against the rules? That's the other part about playing—sometimes making a bit of a mess is half the fun. Even for twelve-year-olds.

As Celeste lay on the bed, I was still obsessing over the Barbie castle. "I swear I could live inside this thing for the rest of my life."

Celeste grinned. "One day I snuck my cat, Harry, over from Uncle Dirk's. We played in there all day and Mom never knew."

Sheesh, I was actually starting to feel sorry for Celeste. No friends over? Sneaking her own cat into her room to play? Talk about sad.

The door opened, and Celeste's mom stuck her head in. "Celeste," she hollered, then entered the room. Her hands were on her hips—never a good sign. "I've been looking all over for you." Her mom's head turned toward me. "Oh, hello. Ivy's friend, right?" Not exactly a friendly welcome.

The next words out of my mouth surprised even me. "I'm Celeste's friend too."

"Right," she said, then turned her attention back

to her daughter. "You need to come down now. The wedding is about to start."

Celeste stood up from her bed and started walking toward her mom.

"Look at your dress!" her mother howled. "It's wrinkled everywhere. I told you to be careful!"

Celeste began to straighten out her dress with her hands. "That won't help," her mother said. "The wrinkles are set. Besides, your hands are probably dirty. You're making it worse."

Celeste looked at her hands, then slowly lowered them along with her head. But her mom hadn't finished. "Stop sulking. We don't have time to do anything about it. You'll just have to go out there with a wrinkled mess." Her mom let out a huge breath and held the bedroom door open wide. Celeste slipped through.

Now Mrs. Holt stared at me, especially my bare feet. I knew they weren't dirty because I'd just taken a bath. Funny thing is, it was obvious she'd been upset with her daughter, but with me, her face turned blank. Empty. I wished she hadn't noticed me so I could crawl inside the Barbie castle for the rest of the afternoon. I'd probably fit. But I quickly slipped on my sandals, held my breath, and slid past Celeste's mom.

The rest of the afternoon was almost a blur—a wedding, people smiling, people happy-crying, people eating and drinking—all outside in the beautiful garden of the beautiful house. After a while I had to use the bathroom, so Ivy and I walked over to Farmer Dirks place. I told her I wanted to see her new bedroom—they'd moved things in yesterday. But the real reason was, I didn't feel comfortable going back into Celeste's house. I didn't feel welcome there.

● ● ● ● ●

Dear Dad,

School went by fast, almost too fast. I only have two months left with Ivy. Don't get me wrong, I'm excited to see you, just sad that I have to move one more time, away from my first-ever, very best friend. It almost doesn't seem fair. Grandma says sometimes life is like a birthday cake without frosting. Grandma is right.

Even though moving away from Ivy makes me sad, seeing you again makes me very happy. Can someone be happy and sad at the same time?

Love, Allie

12

Listening to Goats

The week following the wedding was awful. Ivy and Ty stayed at Celeste's house the entire week while their mom and Farmer Dirk honeymooned in Hawaii—a gift from Celeste's parents. But it was no gift to Ivy and me. Not only were we apart for the entire week, but Ivy was with Celeste. I wasn't sure if I felt sorry for her or me.

By Friday at two I'd cleaned my room, written

a letter to dad, helped Grandma weed the garden, played checkers with Spencer, and counted every crack in the ceiling of my bedroom—twice. How much more boring could my day get?

I was about to go hang out with the goats when Mom handed me the phone.

"Sounds like Ivy."

I grabbed that phone like it was the last piece of chocolate left on planet earth.

"Hello?"

Ivy's voice was low. "Can you meet me at Brown's in about twenty minutes?"

"Why are you whispering?"

"I don't know if I'm supposed to use the phone." She lowered her voice even more. "Lots of rules around this place. Anyway, we're heading to Brown's in just a bit. Mrs. Holt needs some groceries and said we could come for ice cream."

"Okay," I said. "See you there."

"Gotta go." I heard a click and Ivy's voice was gone.

I ran into the kitchen. "Mom, can I go get ice cream at Brown's?"

"Sure," she said. *Wow, that was easy!* "And why don't you take Spencer with you."

"Mom!" I bellowed.

Spencer and his radar ears ran into the kitchen. "I want ice cream."

"Mo-om!" I repeated, this time in two syllables. "I'm meeting Ivy. I haven't seen her all week."

Mom reached for her purse, pulled out a five dollar bill and handed it to me. "Take your brother, please."

When I looked over at Spencer, he reminded me of a puppy dog begging for scraps.

"Come on."

Spencer followed me out the door and we headed to Brown's.

In Edna, there are only a few places to run into friends during the summer—the park, the post office, and Brown's grocery store. That's about it.

Brown's mostly sells groceries, and they even rent DVDs, but my favorite part of the store is up front where they sell ice cream cones. There are twelve flavors in huge tubs. If you're lucky, there's an empty seat at one of the three tables sitting next to the window. It's a favorite spot for kids, especially during the summer months. Grocery shopping moms like it too.

When Spencer and I arrived, we picked out our flavors and sat down. I hadn't taken more than four licks of my mint chocolate chip when the bell on the door rang and Mrs. Holt, Celeste, Ty, and Ivy walked in. Celeste's mom handed her some money before turning toward the shopping carts.

"Allie!" Ivy waved and ran toward me. "I've missed you."

"I've missed you too."

Celeste voice broke in to our little reunion. "Ivy, what flavor do you want?"

"I'll be back," Ivy said and ran over to her brother and Celeste. The three looked through the glass at the colorful tubs of ice cream. They seemed to be having fun, joking, and laughing. It took forever. As I watched, something painful hit me right in the middle of my stomach. Or maybe my heart. Was I jealous of Celeste standing so close to Ty, it looked like their clothes were Velcroed together? Or was I jealous of Celeste and Ivy laughing over something that I couldn't hear?

The answer—*yes!*

When they finally made their selection and sat down, all I had left was the pointy bottom of my cone.

"Hi, Ty," Spencer said. "Got any gum?" I looked over at my brother, chocolate ice cream drizzling down his chin.

I groaned and pushed a pile of napkins toward him.

Ty smiled. "Not today, buddy." He picked up a napkin, reached across the table, and wiped Spencer's chin.

"I'm surprised to see you here," Celeste said to me while scooting her chair closer to Ty's.

"Last I checked, this was still America," I replied, then popped the tip of the cone into my mouth.

Ty and Ivy looked at me like my skin had just turned green.

"I called Allie and told her to meet me here," Ivy said.

Celeste didn't seem fazed as she licked her cone, orange sherbet covering her tongue. She was too busy staring at Ty. Unlike the spaghetti dinner at Farmer Dirk's, Ty seemed to enjoy the attention.

A small stack of flyers at the edge of the table caught my attention. An American flag was at the top. Another reminder of Dad.

Ivy pointed, "What's that?"

I picked up one of the papers and read.

> In 300 words or less, nominate Edna's AMERICAN OF THE YEAR. Eligible entries must be turned into EAOTY committee chair, Harlo Brown, at Brown's Grocery Store by June 15th. The winner is selected by the EAOTY committee and will be announced on July 4th, 12:00 pm at the Edna Independence Day Celebration in the park.

I tossed the paper to Ivy. "Something about an 'Edna American of the Year' contest on the 4th of July."

Ty and Ivy read the flyer. Celeste continued to lick and gawk.

"Maybe we could nominate someone," Ivy said.

"Make it someone old," said Celeste. "Old people win every year."

Ty held up his ice cream cone. "I have an idea," he said. "Why don't you nominate your dad?"

"I don't think he's old enough," Celeste said with a laugh.

Ty shook his head. "No, I meant *Allie's* Dad. He's an American hero. He's been in Iraq for over a year now. He'd be the perfect choice."

A puff of air escaped Celeste lips. What was *that* supposed to mean?

"Maybe I will," I said. I looked into Ty's face. He was nodding and his eyes were wide. They were also very blue. I thought I might melt like the ice cream, dripping again down my brother's chin.

"Let me know if I can help," he said.

I looked at Celeste's face. Stone cold.

"I will," I replied.

I've never been one of those people who have a hard time falling asleep at night—well, except for Christmas Eve and the night before school starts. But I'd been lying up in my attic bedroom for hours and my mind would *not* shut off. Tired of the fight, I stood up and walked over to the window. I crawled up onto the bench seat, pulled back the white curtains, and looked out.

It must have been a full moon because I could see right out into the field behind Grandma's house.

The moonlight gave everything a silver glow. Abe and Chewie slept in front of the chicken coop, their bodies snuggled together, Chewie's head resting against Abe. Good old Abraham Lincoln had turned into a wonderful dad for Chewie. He took good care of him and the two were never apart.

This made me think of my dad all the way in Iraq. He was a good dad too, but we were so far apart. Too far apart. I wanted to snuggle up to Dad and rest my head on his shoulder, but I couldn't. Not yet, anyway.

And when the time came when I finally could, I'd have to leave Edna to do it. Leave Ivy—my only real friend. My best friend.

And then there was Ty. He wasn't my boyfriend or anything like that, but he was always so nice. Always so helpful. Always so . . . *hot!* If I didn't laugh, I was sure I'd cry.

The thought of Ty brought his words back to my mind. *Why don't you nominate your dad?* I stared down at the goats. Even though they were asleep, they seemed to be talking to me—saying the same thing.

I stood up and found my pants across the back of the chair. I searched the pockets till I found the piece of paper. After returning to the window seat, I unfolded the paper. In the moonlight I read the words again.

Nominate Edna's AMERICAN OF THE YEAR.

13

Independence Day

Independence Day changes Edna from a little hick town into one huge outdoor party. The population increases a bazillion times over. From what Grandma told me, everyone who has ever lived in Edna, or knows someone who lives in Edna, comes by for the celebration. There's something for everyone, from a big race in the morning, to a rodeo and fireworks at night. In between there's a ton of stuff happening at the park—pancake breakfast, singers and dancers, barbeque, games, you name it.

I'd spent the entire morning with Ivy. What a blast. We romped around Edna, from the park, to the school playground, to Browns, to the rodeo grounds, and back to the park. Our moms, along with every other adult in Edna, sat in the park, eating, chatting, and watching the local talent. Ivy and I were surprised to find out that my mom knew Farmer Dirk from their school days. He was a few years older, but they remembered each other. And even freakier—Mom knew Celeste's mom. They'd been in the same class the whole time Mom was growing up. They didn't talk for too long, though, so I figured they hadn't been best friends. Not a shocker.

"Why do you keep checking your watch?" Ivy asked as we walked from the swings back to our moms.

"I need to be back to my mom at noon." Which was sort of the truth. Mom never said I *had* to be back then, but I needed to be there, because that's when they'd announce Edna's American of the Year. I'd nominated my dad, so I was a little anxious.

"You did it, didn't you?" Ivy said.

"Did what?"

"You nominated your dad for that Edna's American thingy."

I put my finger to my lips. "Shhhh, I don't want anyone to know."

"Why?"

"Because he probably won't win, and I don't want my mom or Spencer or Grandma or even Ty to get their hopes up."

"Why didn't you tell me? We're best friends."

"I don't know. You've been busy with Celeste."

"Only because our parents keep forcing us to do things together. I can't do anything about that."

"I know. I understand." I said the words, but my heart didn't really believe it. I didn't understand. When Ivy first moved here, she hated Celeste Holt. And now they were next-door neighbors, stepcousins, and hanging out more than either of us wanted to admit. I hated to think about it.

"So what time is it right now?" Ivy asked.

"Five till noon," I said.

Ivy grabbed my arm and we ran toward our moms.

"Now don't say anything," I said.

"I won't, I promise."

When we reached our moms, they were still talking, and still eating. Tommy slept in his stroller, and Spencer sat on the a blanket with another kid about his age.

The park was packed with more people than I'd seen all day. Ty sat on the grass with some seventh grade boys when Celeste, Aubrey, and Tiffany, full of giggles, snaked through the crowd until they found a spot right in front of the guys. Could they be more obvious?

Ivy pointed to an empty spot a few feet behind her brother. "Let's sit there. I think Mr. Brown is about to start."

My stomach hit the ground before my rear end did. Why had I sent in that stupid essay about my dad? No one around here even knew him. Oh well, what did it matter? They'd announce some old person, if you asked Celeste, so I had nothing to worry about.

Harlo Brown, the butcher at Brown's groceries, walked to the microphone set up on a portable stage, and tapped it a few times.

"Ladies and Gentlemen, citizens and friends of Edna, may I have your attention please. It's time to announce Edna's American of the Year."

I wanted to throw up.

When I looked up, something drew my attention to Ty. He had turned around, and those blue eyes were looking right at me. That was when he did it. He winked. At me. With those blue eyes.

Now I needed to both throw up *and* faint.

I looked behind me for a moment, because there was no way in the universe Ty Peterson had winked at *me*, Allie Claybrook. It must have been some cute seventh grade girl behind me. But when I turned back, he smiled. Maybe even laughed a little. Then he faced the stage.

Mr. Brown continued. "Before I reveal this year's winner, I need to announce that the committee has made a slight change this year in its selection process. Along with a winner, we are also announcing an honorary winner. This person wasn't eligible to win because technically he isn't a citizen of Edna. As a matter of fact, right now, he isn't even living in our country. But his wife and children are . . ."

I wondered if anyone would notice if a twelve-year-old girl stood up and ran from the park. No luck—I was blocked in by a sea of bodies.

Mr. Brown chuckled as if he'd said something funny. "Well, I'm getting ahead of myself here. Let's do this properly." He held up a piece of paper. "There's something here I'd like to read, but I suppose it would sound a whole lot better coming from the source who wrote it. Is there a Miss Allison Jayne Claybrook in the crowd?"

Mumbles stirred throughout the park and heads turned in every direction. Ivy nudged my ribs but I couldn't seem to move. Then I heard mom's voice.

"Allie?"

I turned to face her. Her eyes were wide and one hand covered her mouth, while the other wrapped around her stomach, like she needed a hug.

Before I had a chance to even think, someone pulled at my elbow. As I rose to my feet, the audience began to clap and I finally saw who was pulling me up—Ty Peterson, who was now pushing me toward the stage.

As people moved to make a path, Mr. Brown continued. "The committee simply couldn't ignore Miss Claybrook's compelling nomination of her father, Captain James Spencer Claybrook of the United States Army, 20th Engineer Brigade."

The cheers grew louder, giving me energy to walk up onto that stage. And then there was silence. I was staring out at that park-full of faces, with a microphone in one hand, and my nomination essay in the other. I wasn't sure my mouth even worked . . . until I saw mom's face. She was nodding.

I cleared my throat.

"Dear Committee . . ."

I stopped and looked out at the crowd again. Mom was still hugging herself, still nodding. I turned back to the paper.

"I would like to nominate my dad, Captain James Spencer Claybrook of the United States Army, 20th Engineer Brigade to be Edna's American of the Year.

"Some dads like to grow things, so they become farmers. Some dads like to build things, so they become carpenters. Some dads like to be their own boss, so they buy a quarry. My dad is different. He does his job as a soldier in the United States Army because of his beliefs.

"My dad believes that we live in a great nation with freedom to choose. He never wants us to lose that freedom. In some places in this world, bad people take away the freedom from others. My dad is willing to fight for this freedom because he doesn't want me to grow up in a world without it.

"My dad believes the United States was founded by men who had some help from God. Dad says sometimes ideas like this aren't popular, but there are a whole lot more important things in life than being popular. What's most important is being true to yourself. For Dad, this means being a soldier and serving our country.

"Some dads are able to come home every night and tell their kids they love them. My dad can't. He's thousands of miles away in Iraq. But when I want to feel close to him and feel his love, all I have to do is look in the mirror. I am who I am, because my dad taught me to be true to myself. I may not be the most beautiful, or most popular, but I'm me.

"I think my dad would be proud of me, like I'm proud of him. That's why you should choose my dad as Edna's American of the Year.

"Sincerely,

"Allison Jayne Claybrook."

When I finished reading, I lowered my hands and looked out into the crowd. Silence. I didn't know if I should cry, or curtsey, or run off the stage and stick my head in the sandbox.

Before I had a chance to plan my escape route, the entire park erupted—cheering, clapping, screaming, whistling. The sandbox was starting to sound good again. I looked out to see Mom, but she was lost in the crazy mess of cheering people. I had a feeling she was cheering too.

As I walked back out into the crowd, people I didn't even know were smiling at me and patting my back. Mr. Brown announced the official winner and the crowd cheered again.

Ivy waved me back over to our spot, so I sat and then turned to see Mom. Her eyes were red and full of tears, but she was smiling and gave me the thumbs up! I smiled and sat down next to Ivy.

Ivy put her arm around me and squeezed tight. "That was *so good!*"

I was about to say how I felt like a dork up there, but I didn't get a chance. Ty turned around and said three of the most wonderful words I'd ever heard.

"Great job, Allie."

Right then, right there, I was the happiest twelve-year-old girl in the universe.

14

The Bright Side of Midnight

Living in Edna this summer was so much better than the one before. Last summer we'd just arrived, I had no friends, Mom was pregnant with Tommy and sick all the time, and I was forced to hang out with my little brother and a goat. Could it get any worse?

When I found out Dad wasn't coming home from Iraq until July, I almost thought this summer was also ruined. But with Ivy as my best friend, life got better. Except for the week after the wedding, we'd spent all summer together. It was awesome—the best summer of my life.

"I can't believe how much Chewie has grown in the past few months—he's huge," Ivy said. We'd spread a blanket out in Grandma's back field and sat on it while petting the goats. Abe kept his distance, but Chewie (who was used to me because I'd bottle fed him) came right up to us.

I thought it was strange how different two goats could be, and yet, they seemed to love each other. Wherever Abe went, Chewie followed. And if Chewie was ever in any danger (like when he almost escaped through the hole in the fence), Abe was right there to protect him. He was almost like a dad or a big brother to Chewie. They were a put–together family, almost like Ivy's, and they'd become part of my family too.

"It totally stinks that I have to move," I said. "If a goat changes so much in a few months, what do you think will happen to us?"

Neither of us said anything for a moment. The truth of my words pressed down heavy along with the summer sun.

Ivy finally spoke. "We may change a little on

the outside." She looked down at her body. "At least I *hope* I do." We both laughed, but it didn't last.

"What if we change on the inside? What if you totally forget about me?" I wanted to add, *and become best friends with Celeste?* It didn't seem possible now, but Ivy would have to find a friend somewhere. Celeste was right next door. They were technically cousins now.

Ivy tore off a handful of field grass and threw it at me.

"Hey." I shook the grass out of my hair. "What'd ya do that for?"

" 'Cause you're a dork if you think I'm just going to forget about you. Besides, I was thinking. Maybe you could stay and live with your grandma. Lots of kids live with their grandmas."

"I seriously don't think my mom and dad would go for it."

Ivy took a deep breath and let the air slowly pass through her lips. We were both unhappy about this but didn't know how to fix it.

"So whose house are we going to sleep at tonight?" I decided to change the subject. Lucky for us, our moms were letting us do a lot of sleepovers. Now, with only one week till we left for Killeen to see Dad, it was all becoming real. This would be my last week with Ivy until I came to visit Grandma again—hopefully Christmas but most likely next summer. An entire year apart! First Dad, now Ivy. At least we had a few sleepovers left.

Ivy kissed Chewie's head and looked up at me. "Whose house do you want to sleep at?"

"I vote your place. Then we don't have to deal with Spencer."

"True," Ivy said, "but then we have to deal with Ty."

I tried not to smile when Ivy mentioned her brother's name, but the corners of my mouth seemed to curl up on their own whenever anyone mentioned Ty's name. Ugh. Why did my best friend's brother have to be so *hot?* Life was so much simpler when I was Spencer's age and thought all boys had cooties.

Now Ivy was grinning too. "So when are you finally going to admit you have a crush on my brother?"

"I don't."

"Yeah . . . right. Your cheeks turn bright red whenever you're around him."

"I think you're colorblind." Lame comeback, I know, but I was desperate not to let anyone in on my secret, even my best friend. The truth was, I did have a crush on Ty—another tragedy of our leaving.

"Whatever," Ivy said as she pet Chewie's neck. "Then I suppose you don't want to know what he said about you last night."

"Ty said something . . . about *me?*"

Ivy nodded.

"What? Tell me!"

"I thought you didn't like him." Ivy looked happy with herself.

"Will you stop it, and tell me already."

"Okay, okay. He said it was cool that your dad's a soldier—he thinks soldiers are brave."

"That's not about me—it's about my dad."

Ivy put her hand on my shoulder. "There's more—be patient."

"And . . . "

"And he said he really liked your essay about your dad. The one you read on the Fourth of July. He said you were brave."

"He thinks I'm brave?"

"Yeah."

"Brave? That's it?"

"Brave is good."

"Hmmmm . . . " I was disappointed. I'd been hoping for *cute* or *pretty* or even *funny.* But *brave?*

"Actually, Ty wants to be a soldier like your dad someday—so in his book, the term *brave* is right up there with Disneyland, Christmas, and straight A's."

"Well, okay then." It was interesting to find this out. Aside from the deal on the Fourth of July, not too many people here in Edna ever talked to me about my dad. It was almost like he didn't exist except in my memories and through e-mail with him or conversations with Mom, Spencer, Grandma, or Ivy—she wasn't afraid to bring him up like other people seemed to be.

The truth was that Dad *did* exist. And he was one of the bravest men I ever knew. If Ty wanted to be like my dad someday, then he was brave too— another thing to admire about Ty Peterson.

That night Ivy's mom agreed to let us sleep in sleeping bags out on the trampoline. The only catch—Celeste had to sleep over too. Celeste's mom and dad were staying out late and didn't want her to be home alone. Puh-leeze! I think they wanted to torture me.

Aside from the extra company, it was a beautiful Idaho summer night—especially in Ivy's new backyard. Since Farmer Dirk's house was out in the country, the stars seemed extra bright.

"Now where is it again you're moving to?" Ivy asked.

"North Carolina—Fort Bragg"

Ivy slapped her hand on the trampoline, sending a vibration that rippled underneath us. "That's so far away. We'll never see each other."

Celeste's black cat, Harry, had been sitting in her arms, but was startled by Ivy. It hissed and jumped at the same time, landing on the grass.

"Thanks a lot," Celeste said, with her own hiss

and jumped off to get the cat. I suppose we should have helped, but we were too depressed.

"Better put Harry back in the house," Ivy suggested.

"I'm going to," Celeste hollered back. "I don't want you freaking him out again."

I rolled my eyes, but nobody saw. How could I possibly leave Ivy here with Celeste? It just wasn't fair to either of us.

I tried to take Grandma's advice and find the bright side of midnight in our situation, but honestly, there weren't many. "We've both gotten pretty good at e-mail lately. We can keep in touch that way. And phone calls. At least until I come back next summer."

"True, but it won't be the same."

"I know." I looked up at that jumble of mixed-up stars in the sky and figured I was looking at my own jumbled thoughts at the moment. Part of me was like those really bright stars beaming as bright as I could because I'd be seeing my dad in only one more week. I'd waited for so long—it almost didn't seem real.

But then another part, a *really big* part, felt like the black spaces between those stars—dark, empty, nothing there but cold space. I was losing my best friend and the home we'd created over the past year.

At first I hated Edna. It was different than any place I knew. There weren't a lot of people, that's for sure. And no one else was in the army, at least that I knew of. Back in Killeen, whenever we went to Wal-Mart or just about anywhere, half the adults walking around were soldiers dressed in cammies. I almost thought it was like that everywhere else until I came to Edna. Now this place was my normal. My home.

Like I said, my mind was mixed up. I suppose all I could do was close my eyes and wait for the sun to come up. Maybe then I'd see things better.

I'd always been one to have slightly crazy dreams. There was the flying one—all I had to do was flap my arms and up into the sky I went. And then the one where I wore pajamas to school. Totally embarrassing. I don't even want to think about the ones involving spiders. They're the worst because they seem so real.

So when I was in that fuzzy place I often find myself waking up to, I was surprised that the smell from my dream was stuck in my memory. In my dream, I'd been making cookies with Grandma over a campfire. Don't ask me why. Obviously cookies need to be baked in an oven—even *I* knew that. But not in this dream. Grandma and I were making her chewy chocolate chip cookies like you might make pancakes over a campfire. Whatever.

My back was feeling a little uncomfortable for some reason, so I rolled over. The surface under me quivered with the movement, and it was only then that I remembered I was sleeping on a trampoline outside Ivy's house. So why was I smelling that campfire still?

I sat up, stretched a bit, then rubbed my eyes. As the sleeping bag fell from my shoulders, the brisk air brushed across my arms and neck, causing the hairs to raise. Through the moonlight I could see Celeste and Ivy, snoozing next to me. Celeste was even snoring.

But there was another sound, unfamiliar to the night. And that smell . . .

I looked around—the rows of potato plants in the field, Celeste's big rock house down the road, that big tree in her backyard. Amazing how the moon lit up the night. But that unfamiliar smell returned, forcing my attention in another direction—Ivy's house. The lights were all out except for at the far right. I think that's where her garage was. A flickering of yellow-orange light sparked through the window sending a signal to my brain.

"Ivy—fire." I was screaming inside, but my voice sounded weak to my ears—like I was still in a dream. A nightmare! How could there possibly be a fire in Ivy's garage? We'd just been in there a few hours earlier, taking out trash. I shook both Ivy and Celeste.

Ivy rolled over. "What?" Her voice was dry. Celeste sat up too.

"Your house—fire." I pointed to the flicker of light through the garage window.

"Oh no!" Ivy jumped off the trampoline, and Celeste and I were right behind her. We ran barefoot to the edge of the yard near the side of the house. That was no campfire. Flames were licking at the garage window.

Ivy took a step toward the flames, but I grabbed her hand, pulling her back. "We gotta wake up your mom and Dirk and Ty."

She nodded and we both ran toward her back door. Celeste was already in. The minute we were inside Ivy started yelling. "Mom! Dirk! Fire!"

Dirk stumbled into the hall, followed by Ivy's mom, and then Ty.

"What—what's wrong?" Dirk said.

Now Ivy was crying, so I spoke.

"A fire. In the garage."

Everyone's attention shifted from the two of us to the back door. Ivy's mom grabbed the phone as we all ran out.

I pulled the neck of my t-shirt over my nose. The smell of smoke was much stronger in the house. Dirk hollered back to Ivy's mom, "Call 911. And then call Mark and Connie. You kids stay back. Go next door."

I could hear Ivy's mom on the phone, hear the panic in her voice, see the fear in her eyes. All by moonlight.

We'd done pretty good on the "staying back" part until we saw Mrs. Holt running toward us, wearing her nightgown and robe. Ivy's mom ran toward her and the two hugged.

"Where's Celeste?" Mrs. Holt asked when the two pulled apart.

"She didn't run home?" asked Ivy's mom. Then she turned to us. "Girls?"

We both looked around. Ty was standing there with the two of us, but not Celeste. "She was with us," Ivy said. "Just a minute ago . . . when we went in to wake everyone up."

Ivy's mom looked panicked. "I didn't see her."

"She went into the burning house?" Mrs. Holt was screaming now.

A memory of Celeste's came to mind. "I bet she's looking for her cat," I said.

Mr. Holt ran up beside his wife. "Where's Celeste?"

"She's in the house . . . looking for that cat." Mrs. Holt was screaming and coughing at the same time. I'd never seen such panic in someone's eyes.

Mr. Holt sprinted toward the burning house. Farmer Dirk was spraying the house with a hose. When Celeste's dad approached, he dropped the hose, and the two ran toward the back door. And that was when Ty ran toward the burning house.

"Get back here!" Ivy's mom yelled.

"I know where the cat is." He hollered over his shoulder.

"Ty—"

He didn't turn around, just kept running toward the blaze. It was growing. Flames crawled up the garage door. The garage window was lit up like a fireplace on a cold December night. But it was July. And that was no fireplace.

Celeste's mom was near hysterical. "What if they can't find her? My baby . . . " She let out a sound I didn't even know—part cry, part moan, maybe even part growl. She started to collapse but Ivy's mom held her up.

I thought about Celeste and that black cat she seemed to love so much. She'd told me once it was her best friend. Was it true? Where was she, and where was that stupid black cat? Now I was crying.

My heart felt like it was pounding in my head. I covered my ears to stop the noise but it didn't work. I didn't want Celeste or even that cat to die in the fire.

As I looked over to the house, I tried to see if the flames had spread into the rest of the house. With all the smoke, I couldn't tell.

Ivy pointed toward the burning house. "Someone's coming."

It was Farmer Dirk, running toward us, hands cupped around his mouth. "Is she there? Did she come out?"

"No," we all hollered back.

Ivy's stepdad didn't stop to talk, just spun around and ran back toward his burning house.

"Where's the fire department?" Ivy asked her mom.

"They're coming," she replied.

"I need to go back . . . to look for Celeste." Mrs. Holt was sobbing. "Maybe she's afraid. Maybe she's hiding."

Ivy's mom kept an arm around the crying woman. "She's too old for that. Besides, Dirk and Mark will find her."

Our attention was quickly drawn to the sirens of the fire trucks. Finally! It felt like forever since Ivy's mom had called.

The moment seemed to get even crazier with the arrival of the fire trucks. Men in firefighter gear began hauling hoses toward the house. The flames began to extend beyond the garage, and a fear I'd never before felt settled in. Where was

Celeste? And now Ty? It felt like hours since I woke up on the trampoline.

Mrs. Holt pulled away from Ivy's mom and ran toward the firemen in her nightgown. She was still screaming and crying, but it was hard to hear her over the commotion. She was pointing to the burning house as she pulled on the fireman's arm.

Ivy's mom wrapped her arms around us, and it wasn't until that moment that I even realized how cold I was. My teeth chattered and my entire body shook. Ivy's mom must have noticed because she pulled us both in tight.

As we stared at the chaos, I heard Mrs. Holt scream. Then she began to run toward the house.

No! I thought. *Don't go in there too.* But when I looked through the haze of the smoke to where she was headed, I saw several figures walking toward us. With each step away from the smoke, the scene became clearer.

Dirk held his arm around Ty's shoulder as the two approached. Ivy's mom dropped her arms from around us and lifted her hands to her face as she cried softly.

Behind them, Mr. Holt was carrying Celeste. One arm clung to his neck while the other held on tight to Harry, the black cat. It wasn't until she heard her mom's cry that Celeste dropped to her feet and ran into her mother's arms.

She was okay!

As the fire blazed in the background, I watched the silhouette of Mr. Holt pulling both his wife and daughter into his strong arms. It looked like it might take a hundred firemen to release his hold on his family. They didn't look like they wanted to be anywhere else.

Then I glanced to the right. Ivy's family was also huddled together. And even though I knew Farmer Dirk was her stepdad, it didn't seem to make a difference. The four of them were in some sort of football huddle-of-hugs.

As I watched these families share their love with each other, I only wanted one thing—to be home. And that was any place I was with the people I loved most.

My family.

● ● ● ● ●

Dear Dad,

I miss you so much! More than anything, I want our family to be together again—even if we have to move to North Carolina or the North Pole!

I love you!

Cracker Jack

15

Welcome Home, Baghdaddy!

I'd waited fourteen months, rode three days in a car with a screaming seven-month-old baby brother, even got a haircut and wore a new dress, and all for today. All for Dad.

He was coming home from Iraq today and, well, I'd have done about anything except wait another minute to have Dad home again. Now that the time was here—we were here—it almost didn't seem real.

All the families, about a bazillion of us, gathered in a huge gym. I saw a few friends from my old school. Now *that* was a little weird. Everyone looked different. Everyone had changed—especially me. We all knew it.

I wondered if Dad would recognize me. I wondered if he'd love me as much now as he did when he left. Grandma says, "If you love 'em every day, you'll love 'em more when they're away." Sometimes I had to wonder where Grandma came up with all her crazy sayings. Funny thing is, when you think about the words, they're always true.

I missed Grandma and Ivy. But I'd see them again. Maybe Christmas. For sure next summer. We also had e-mail, phone calls, and lots of great memories to keep our friendship strong forever.

Loud music played over speakers as families waved homemade banners on posters and sheets: *We love Dad; We missed you Mom;* and *Welcome home Baghdaddy*—that was my favorite!

Spencer, wearing Dad's favorite black baseball cap, tugged on Mom's arm. "When do we get to see him?"

"Any minute now," she replied. I think she'd said it ten times already and probably wanted it more than any of us. Tommy was fussing in her arms, but he didn't want anyone else, only Mom.

The heat didn't help either. What can you expect for Texas in July and in a room buzzing with people? Funny thing was, aside from the babies who had no clue what was going on, everyone else was probably happier than they'd been in over a year.

"Here they come!" a voice hollered. The buzz grew louder. The excitement, stronger. If I closed my eyes, I was sure I could reach out and touch it—be shocked by the air—that's how crazy everything felt. Crazy good!

Before I even realized what was happening, soldiers began running into the room from the far end. We all cheered, stood on tippy-toes, and squinted, trying to figure out which soldier belonged to us. It was almost impossible to tell, and a fear shot through me that maybe they forgot Dad. Maybe he was back in Iraq.

"I think I see him!" Mom squealed. She was way excited—even wore the red dress dad loved so much.

"Are you sure?" I asked, and squinted harder. The soldiers lined up in formation, and from where I stood, you couldn't tell one from another.

Someone hollered out orders to the soldiers, and I felt like hollering, "All right, already! You've had him for fourteen months. It's my turn. *I WANT MY DAD—NOW!*"

As soon as I said, *"NOW!"*—only in my mind,

of course—a roar shot out from the group of soldiers as they were released from their duties to find their families. There were tears and squeals as families reunited.

Mom had given Spencer and me strict orders to stick right next to her during all of this. "Too easy to wander off and get lost," she said. But it seemed impossible to find Dad through the commotion.

Frustrated, I stood up on a chair not far from Mom and scanned the room. There were people hugging, people crying, and people laughing. There were lots of dads reuniting with their families, but none of them were my dad.

My throat began to tighten, and my eyes started to sting. Where was he? We drove all the way from Edna—three whole days—to be here to meet Dad. And now what? What if he's not here? For some reason, I found myself praying as I stood there on that chair in that gym full of people, turning slow circles. *Please don't tell me that there was a mistake. Please don't tell me that he's still back in Iraq. Please, please . . .*

"Cracker Jack."

I stood frozen on the chair, afraid to turn around. Afraid it might not be true. Did someone else's dad call her Cracker Jack because he thought she was always full of surprises?

But I knew that voice.

I turned around, and there he was. My dad! He

ran toward me with his hands raised up, and even though I was twelve years old, and way too big, I jumped off of that chair and landed right into Dad's arms as he spun me in circles.

I held tight for a long time. So did he. We had fourteen months of missed hugs to make up for. I'd never felt happier in all my life than I did at that moment. Dad was home. And so was I.

●　●　●　●　●

Dear Ivy,

Hey—guess what? The Grand Canyon is gynormous—bigger than all of Edna, Idaho! It's great to be together again with my dad, but I really miss you!

How was your trip to California? You and Ty were so lucky to fly on an airplane to see your dad. I'm always stuck riding in The Bruise. We're on our way to Fort Bragg, North Carolina right now. Even though I hope I make new friends at my new home, no one will ever replace you—the best best friend ever!

See you next summer!

Love, Allie—your best friend forever.

P.S. I hope your house is rewired and rebuilt soon. Sorry your family has to live with Celeste for the next month. Personally, I'd move into the Barbie castle with the cat. I'm glad her mom let Harry move back in!

Character and Setting

In a book, the characters are the people in a story. A character could even be an animal. Every character has a different role in the story. There are many terms or names used for characters in a story.

Main Character: This is the person who the book is mostly about. This person is often called the **protagonist**, or the "good guy." Sometimes they tell the story in their own voice. This is called **first person point of view.**

- Who is the Main Character in *Make Me a Home?*
- Is the story told in first person point of view?

Supporting Character: This is someone often seen in the story, but who doesn't have as large of a part as the main character. Often, a supporting character is a friend of the main character or protagonist.

- Name a supporting character in *Make Me a Home.*
- What is their relationship to the main character?

Antagonist: This is usually the person in a story who creates opposition for the main character/protagonist. They are often seen as the "bad guy" in the story.

- Who is the antagonist in *Make Me a Home?*
- Can you think of more than one?

Setting: This is the location where the story takes place. Sometimes a setting is a real place, and sometimes it is fictitious (made up).

- What is the setting of *Make Me a Home?*
- Is this setting a real place or is it fictitious?

Discussion Questions

Why do Allie, her mom, and her little brothers live in Edna, Idaho, with their grandma?

How does Allie feel about living in Edna, Idaho?

How does Allie feel when she learns her dad has to stay in Iraq for two extra months?

How does Allie feel when Ivy Peterson moves into town?

What is the one thing (besides having her dad home) that Allie wants more than anything while living in Edna, Idaho?

How are Allie and Ivy similar? How are they different?

Have you ever had a best friend? What does it mean to have a best friend?

Who is Farmer Dirk? What is his relationship to Ivy and Celeste?

How does Grandma's goat, Abraham Lincoln, feel about Chewie, the baby goat? Is there a similarity between the goats' relationship and any characters in this story?

What is unique about Allie's grandma?

Can you name one of her unique sayings? Does it sound similar to a saying you have heard before?

What event took place in the school cafeteria between Allie and Celeste? How did it change the remainder of the school year for the two girls?

How are Allie and Celeste different? How are they similar?

Does Allie get to know Celeste better by the end of the story? Have you ever met someone you didn't like at first, but after you got to know them better, they became your friend?

What does Allie write and then read at the Edna Independence Day celebration?

How does Allie feel about her dad? Who is your hero? Why?

What happens the night Allie and Celeste have a sleepover outside on Ivy's trampoline?

How does Allie feel when she sees Celeste and Ivy hugging their families?

How does Allie feel when she finally reunites with her dad?

Allie has lived in many different places. Where does she finally decide that home is?

Sayings

When I first wrote *Make Me a Home*, Allie's grandma was full of sayings, but they were all cliché. A cliché is a sentence or phrase that we've heard over and over. It's not original, and it's very predictable because we've heard it so often. I loved the character of Grandma and felt that she deserved better, so I decided to make her sayings original—and actually, this was quite challenging at times! Sometimes I changed a word or two from the original cliché. Sometimes I made up a whole new saying. For example:

Early Draft	**Final Draft**
We're two peas in a pod.	We're two beans in a burrito.
First things first.	Worst things first.
Why don't we sleep on it?	Why don't we take it to bed and hope we don't squish it in the middle of the night?
Absence makes the heart grow fonder.	If you love 'em every day, you'll love 'em more when they're away."

Now it's your turn! Below are some famous sayings. What do they mean? Can you change them into something original?

I missed getting an A on the test *by the skin of my teeth.*

Johnny is *the new kid on the block.*

It's *raining cats and dogs* outside.

She's been playing that new game *twenty-four seven.*

When the new Harry Potter book was released, it *hit the ground running.*

I felt like I would explode with excitement if I didn't *let the cat out of the bag.*

Fire Facts

- 80 percent of all fire deaths occur in the home (U.S. Fire Administration).
- A fire doubles in size every minute (safehome. com).
- The leading cause of fire deaths is careless smoking (U.S. Fire Administration).
- Having a working smoke detector more than doubles your chance of surviving a fire (U.S. Fire Administration).

Having only one smoke detector is NOT enough for most houses! Every home should be equipped with smoke detectors on every level, particularly outside of sleeping areas. Change the batteries twice a year, and test it monthly. Also, know what your fire alarm sounds like. It's the sound that saves lives.

Have a Plan!

Does your family have a home fire escape plan? If not, it's time to make one.

- Draw a floor plan showing at least two ways out of each room.
- Sleep with the bedroom doors closed to help hold back the heat and smoke.
- Should you be caught in smoke, **crawl!** Smoke rises, so stay close to the floor.
- Choose a specific place outside for every family member to meet.
- Phone the Fire Department from a **neighbor's house.**
- Make sure no one goes back inside!
- Practice, practice, practice . . . with the whole family.

Friendship Games and Activities

Three Things About Me

Each person in a group takes a turn telling three things that are unique about themselves (something everyone wouldn't already know). But, *only two* of these things can be true, and one thing is made up, or false. After each person states their three things, the group decided which thing the person made up.

Getting to Know You

Everyone is given a paper with different categories on it, such as:

- Never been ice skating
- Born in a state other than (insert name of state where you live)
- Only child in their family
- Read all 7 Harry Potter books
- Been to Disney Land (or Disney World, or any designated theme park)
- Caught a fish

Each player must find someone different to fit into each of the categories and get his or her signature on their papers.

Friendship Bingo

Each child receives a blank Bingo card. Have the children get names of other children and write them in each square. Instead of the caller calling "B3," they will be calling "Jason Brown." Five in a row wins, or you could play 4 Corners or Blackout.

Dear Reader,

As I write these books about Allie (who is only a fictional character, but feels very real to me), my heart fills with gratitude for the members of our U.S. armed forces as well as their family members. These dedicated American citizens (often our next door neighbors) give so much, sometimes everything, to serve our great country and defend the freedoms our forefathers established. To me, they have the true characteristics of a hero.

I often wonder what I can do, as I try to be a good citizen. Most of us aren't required to make the sacrifices of our military families. But I do believe we can make a difference in our communities, and perhaps even in our nation and world by following the four steps of a HERO:

- *Be **H**elpful*
- *Be an **E**xample*
- *Be **R**esponsible*
- ***O**pen our eyes*

I encourage you to discuss these steps in your classroom and with your family and friends. Discover what being a true HERO means to you!

Sincerely,
Tamra Norton

About the Author

Tamra Norton is the author of six published novels for teens and children. Her children's novel *Make Me a Memory* was selected by the Utah Commission on Literacy as the state's prestigious "Book of the Month" for April 2006.

As the mother of seven children (ages five to twenty-two—all homeschooled, with the oldest three now in college), Tamra considers herself a full-time keeper of the peace, feeder of things that growl, and supreme commander of all things coming and going from her home in Spring, Texas. When she isn't gazing vacantly into the computer screen in the middle of the night, she enjoys reading in the bathtub, dancing in the kitchen, camping in the living room, taking an afternoon nap, and eating chocolate. She is a member of SCBWI (Society of Children's Book Writers and Illustrators) and LDStorymakers. You can read more about Tamra and her books at www.tamranorton.com.